THE LAST OF
THE ALDINIS

~ novels and novellas by the same author ~

Rose and Blanche (1831)
(*jointly with Jules Sandeau*)
Indiana (1832)
Valentine (1832)
Lavinia (1833)
Lélia (1834)
The Marquise (1834)
The Private Secretary (1834)
Jacques (1834)
Leone Leoni (1835)
André (1835)
Simon (1836)
Mauprat (1837)
The Mosaic Masters (1838)
The Uscoque (1838)
The Last of the Aldinis (1839)
Spiridion (1839)
Pauline (1839)
The Seven Strings of Her Lyre (1840)
The Companion of the Tour of France (1840)
Horace (1842)
Consuelo (1842-43)
The Countess of Rudolstadt (1844)
Jeanne (1844)
Letters to Marcie (1844)
The Miller of Angibault (1845)
Teverino (1845)
The Sin of Monsieur Antoine (1845)
The Devil's Pool (1846)
Isidora (1846)
Lucrezia Floriani (1846)
The Piccinino (1847)
François the Waif (1847-48)
Little Fadette (1849)
The Castle in the Wilderness (1851)
The Marriage of Victorine (1851)
The Master Pipers (1853)

Mont-Revêche (1853)
The Goddaughter (1853)
Adriani (1854)
The Devil in the Fields (1856)
Évenor and Leucippe (1856)
Daniella (1857)
The Gallant Lords of Boix-Doré (1858)
The Snow Man (1858)
He and She (1859)
Narcisse (1859)
Flavie (1859)
The Marquis of Villemer (1860)
Jean de la Roche (1860)
Constance Verrier (1860)
The Black City (1860)
Valvèdre (1861)
The Germandre Family (1861)
Tamaris (1862)
Antonia (1862)
Mademoiselle la Quintinie (1863)
The Green Women (1863)
Laura (1864)
The Confession of a Young Girl (1865)
Monsieur Sylvestre (1865)
The Last Love (1867)
Cadio (1868)
Mademoiselle Merquem (1868)
A Rolling Stone (1870)
Césarine Dietrich (1871)
Francia (1872)
Handsome Laurence (1872)
Nanon (1872)
Tales of a Grandmother (1873)
My Sister Jeanne (1874)
Flamarande (1874)
The Two Brothers (1875)
Marianne (1876)
The Tower of Percemont (1876)

THE LAST OF THE ALDINIS

by

GEORGE SAND

translated by
GEORGE BURNHAM IVES

SANDNESS
MICHAEL WALMER
2024

The Last of the Aldinis first published in French 1839
This translation first published 1900
This edition published in 2024

by

Michael Walmer
North House
Melby
Sandness
Shetland ZE2 9PL

ISBN 978-0-6457519-2-5 paperback

INTRODUCTION

Novels are always works of the fancy to some extent, and some of the fanciful conceits of the imagination are like clouds that pass over our heads. Whence come the clouds, and whither do they go?

Walking through the forest of Fontainebleau one day, with my son, I dreamed about something very different from this book, which I wrote that same evening in a tavern, and forgot the next morning, to think only of flowers and butterflies. I could describe minutely all our walks and all our amusements, but it is impossible for me to say why my mind flitted to Venice that evening. I might look about for a good reason, but it is more honest to confess that I remember nothing about it. It was some fifteen or sixteen years ago.

GEORGE SAND

Nohant, August 23, 1853

To SIGNORA CARLOTTA MARLIANI

CONSULESSA DI SPAGNA

The sailors of the Adriatic do not launch a new vessel until it is embellished with the image of the Virgin. May your name, written upon this page, O my dear and lovely friend, be like the effigy of the divine patron saint, which protects a fragile bark abandoned to the capricious waves.

GEORGE SAND

FIRST PART

At the time of this story, Signor Lelio was no longer in the first bloom of youth; whether because his lungs, by dint of performing their duty with generous zeal, had developed in such a way as to distend the muscles of his chest, or because of the great care with which singers look after the preservation of the organ of melody, his body, which he jocosely called the *casket* of his voice, had acquired a reasonable degree of embonpoint. His leg, however, had retained all the elegance of its shape, and the habitual grace of all his movements made him still what the ladies, under the empire, called a *beau cavalier*.

But if Lelio was still able to fill the post of *leading man* on the boards of La Fenice and La Scala, without offending good taste or the probabilities; if his still beautiful voice and his great talent maintained him in the first rank of Italian artists; if his abundant locks, of a beautiful pearl-gray, and his great black eye, still full of fire, continued to attract the glances of the gentler sex, in salons as well as upon the stage, it is none the less true that Lelio was a prudent man, most reserved and grave on occasion. A fact that will seem strange to us is that, with all the charms which heaven had bestowed upon him, with the brilliant triumphs of his honorable career, he was not and had never been a libertine. He had, it was said, inspired great passions; but whether because he had never shared them, or because he had buried his romantic experiences in the oblivion of a generous conscience, no one could say what the result had been of any of those mysterious episodes in his life. The fact was that he had never compromised any woman. The wealthiest and most illustrious houses of Italy and Germany welcomed him cordially; he had never introduced scandal or discord into any one of them. Everywhere he enjoyed the reputation of a loyal, good-hearted man, whose virtue was beyond reproach.

To us artists, too, his friends and companions, he was the best and most lovable of men. But that serene cheerfulness, that kindly charm which characterized him in his intercourse with society, did not altogether conceal from us a background of melancholy and the existence of a secret sorrow of long standing. One evening, after supper, as we were smoking under our fragrant arbor at Sainte-Marguerite, Abbé Panorio talked to us of himself, and described the poetic impulses and heroic combats of his own heart with a touching candor worthy of all respect. Lelio, led on by his example and infected by the generally effusive spirit of the party, pressed also in some degree by the abbé's questions and Beppa's glances, confessed to us at last that his art was not the only noble passion he had known.

"*Ed io anchè!*" he exclaimed, with a sigh; "I too have loved, and fought, and triumphed!"

"Had you taken a vow of chastity, pray, as he had?" queried Beppa, with a smile, touching the abbé's arm with the end of her black fan.

"I never took any vow," replied Lelio; "but I have always been irresistibly guided by a natural feeling of justice and truth. I have never understood how one could be truly happy for a single day while compromising another person's future. I will tell you, if you please, the story of two periods of my life in which love played the leading rôle, and you will understand that it cost me a little something to be, I do not say a hero, but a man."

"That is a very solemn beginning," said Beppa, "and I fear that your story will resemble a French sonata! You require a musical introduction, so wait a moment! Does this key suit you?"

As she spoke she struck a chord or two on her lute, and played the first measures of an *andante maestoso* by Dusseck.

"That is not the thing," said Lelio, stifling the notes of the lute with Beppa's fan. "Play me rather one of those German waltzes in which Joy and Sorrow, in a voluptuous embrace, seem to turn slowly round and round, and to display in turn a pale tear-stained face and a radiant brow crowned with flowers."

"Very good!" said Beppa. "Meanwhile Cupid plays the kit, and marks time falsely, exactly like a master of the ballet; Joy impatiently stamps her foot to incite the torpid musician who restrains her impetuosity; Sorrow, utterly exhausted, turns her moist eyes upon the pitiless fiddler to urge him to slacken that incessant whirling about, and the audience, uncertain whether to laugh or cry, concludes to go to sleep."

And Beppa began the *ritornello* of a sentimental waltz, playing the measures fast and slow alternately, making the expression of her charming face, now glistening with joy, now doleful beyond words, conform to that ironical mode of execution, and putting forth in that musical mockery all the energy of her artistic patriotism.

"You are a narrow-minded creature!" said Lelio,

passing his fingers over the strings, whose vibration died away in a shrill, ear-piercing wail.

"No German organ!" cried the fair Venetian, laughing heartily and abandoning the instrument to him.

"The artist's fatherland," said Lelio, "is the whole world, the great *Bohemia,* as we say. *Per Dio!* make war if you please on Austrian despotism, but let us respect the German waltz! Weber's waltzes, O my friends! Beethoven's waltzes and Schubert's! Oh! listen, listen to this poem, this drama, this scene of despair, of passion and delirious joy!"

As he spoke, the artist touched the chords of the lute, and began to sing with all the force of his voice and soul Beethoven's sublime *Desire;* then, abruptly breaking off and throwing the still vibrating instrument on the grass, he said:

"No song ever stirred my heart like that one. We may as well confess that our Italian music appeals only to the senses or to the over-heated imagination; that music speaks to the heart, to the most profound and most exquisite sentiments. I was once like you, Beppa. I resisted the power of German genius; for a long time I closed my bodily ears and the ears of my intelligence to these Northern melodies, which I neither could nor would understand. But the time has come when divine inspiration is no longer called upon to halt on the frontiers of states by reason of the color of its uniform or the pattern of its standards. There are in the air I know not what angels or sylphs, invisible messengers of progress, who bring us melody and poetic thoughts from all points of the compass. Let us not bury ourselves under our own ruins; but let our genius spread its wings and open its arms to espouse all the contemporaneous geniuses beyond the Alps."

"Listen to him! how he raves!" cried Beppa, wiping

her lute which was already wet with dew ; "and I took him for a reasonable man!"

"For a cold, perhaps a selfish man, eh, Beppa?" rejoined the artist with a melancholy air, as he sat down. "Well, I myself have at times believed that I was such a man ; for I have done some reasonable things, and I have made some sacrifices to the demands of society. But when in the evening the bands of the Austrian regiments wake the echoes of our great squares and our placid canals, with airs from *Der Freischutz* and fragments of Beethoven's symphonies, then I find that I have tears in abundance, and that my sacrifices have been worth but little. A new sense seems to awake within me : the sadness of regret and a longing for reverie, elements which seldom enter into our southern character, find their way into my system through every pore, and I see clearly enough that our music is incomplete, and that the art which I serve is insufficient to express the impulses of my heart; that is why I am, as you see, disgusted with the stage, surfeited with the excitement of triumph, and in nowise desirous to win fresh applause by the old methods ; I would like to plunge into a life full of new emotions, and find in the lyric drama an image of the drama of my whole life ; but in that case I should perhaps become as gloomy and despondent as a Hamburger, and you would laugh at me without pity, Beppa ! That must not be. Let us drink, my good friends ! *viva* merry Italy and Venice the fair !"

He put his glass to his lips, then absent-mindedly replaced it on the table without swallowing a drop of wine. The abbé answered him with a sigh, Beppa pressed his hand, and after a few moments of melancholy silence, Lelio, being urged to fulfil his promise, began his narrative in these words :

I am, as you know, the son of a fisherman of Chioggia. Almost all the people along that shore have a well developed thorax and a powerful voice. Their voices would be beautiful if they did not ruin them early in life on their boats by trying to drown the roar of the sea and the wind, and by drinking and smoking beyond all reason, to avoid drowsiness and fatigue. We Chioggiotes are a fine race. It is said that a great French painter, *Leopoldo Roberto,* is even now engaged in commemorating our type of beauty in a picture which he allows nobody to see.

Although I am of a reasonably robust organization, as you see, my father, on comparing me with my brothers, deemed me so frail and sickly that he would not teach me either to cast the net or to sail a boat. He simply showed me how to handle the oar with both hands, to row a small boat, and sent me to Venice to earn my living as an assistant gondolier for hire. It was a great sorrow and humiliation to me, thus to go into bondage, to leave my father's house, the sea-shore and the honorable and perilous trade of my ancestors. But I had a fine voice, I knew a goodly number of fragments of Ariosto and Tasso. I had in me the making of an excellent gondolier, and with time and patience, I might earn fifty francs a month in the service of artists and strangers.

You do not know, Zorzi—at this point Lelio broke off his narrative and turned to me—you have no idea how rapidly the taste and appreciation of music and poetry develop among us common people. We had then and we still have—although the custom threatens to die out— our troubadours and poets, whom we call *cupids;* itinerant rhapsodists they are, and they bring us from the central provinces inaccurate notions of the mother-tongue, modified, I might more properly say enriched, by all the genius of the dialects of the north and south. Men of the people, like ourselves, endowed at once with memory and imaginative power, do not hesitate at all to blend their curious improvisations with the creations of the poets. Forever picking up and dropping as they pass some novel turn of phrase, they embellish their speech and the text of their authors with a most extraordinary confusion of idioms. We might say that they preserve the instability of the language in the frontier provinces and along the coast. In our ignorance we accept as decisive the decisions of this itinerant academy; and you have often had occasion to admire, sometimes the energy, sometimes the grotesqueness of the Italian of our ports as rendered by the singers of the lagoons.

On a Sunday at noon, after high mass, in the public square of Chioggia, or in the evening, in the wine-shops on the shore, these rhapsodists, by their recitations interspersed with bits of singing and declamation, hold spellbound large and enthusiastic audiences. Ordinarily the *cupid* stands on a table, and from time to time plays a prelude or a finale of his own composition on some sort of an instrument; one on the Calabrian bagpipe, another on the Bergamo viol, others on the violin, flute or guitar. The Chioggians, outwardly phlegmatic and cold, listen at first with an impassive and almost contemptuous air, smoking vigorously; but at the mighty lance-thrusts of Ariosto's heroes, at the death of the paladins, at the adventures of damsels delivered and giants run through, the audience is roused, takes fire, shouts and works itself into such a frenzy that glasses and pipes are shivered, tables and chairs smashed, and often the *cupid,* on the point of falling a victim to the excitement aroused by himself, is forced to fly, while the enthusiasts scatter through the fields, in pursuit of an imaginary ravisher, shouting:

"*Amazza! amazza!* kill the monster! kill the rascal! death to the brigand! bravo, Astolphe! courage, my good fellow! forward! forward! kill! kill!"—And so the Chioggians, drunk with tobacco smoke, wine and poetry, rush aboard their boats and declaim to the waves and the winds scattered fragments of those soul-stirring epics.

I was the least noisy and the most attentive of these enthusiasts. As I was very regular in my attendance at the performances, and as I always went away silent and thoughtful, my parents concluded that I was a docile, simple-minded youth, desirous but incapable of learning the noble arts. They considered my voice pleasant to hear; but, as my tendency was toward purer accentuation and less frenzied declamation than the *cupids* and their imitators, they decreed that, as a singer no less than as a boatman, I was *good for the city*—thus reversing your French saying with respect to things of small value : *good for the country*.

I promised to tell you of two episodes only, not the whole story of my life. So I will not detail all the sufferings through which I passed before attaining the age of fifteen years and a very moderate degree of skill as a gondolier, having subsisted meanwhile on rice and water and blows of the oar across my shoulders. The only pleasure I had was in listening to the serenaders; and, when I had a moment's leisure, I would run after the musicians and follow them all over the city. That pleasure was so intense that, even if it did not prevent my sighing for my father's house, it would have prevented me from returning to it. However, my passion for music had reached the point of sympathetic enjoyment only, not of a personal inclination; for my voice was just changing and seemed to me so unpleasant when I ventured timidly to try it, that I looked forward to no other future than that of beating the water of the lagoons all my life, at the service of the first comer.

My master and I often occupied the *traghetto,* or gondola stand, on the Grand Canal in front of the Aldini Palace, near the image of *Saint Zandegola*—a patois contraction of San Giovanni Decollato. While we were waiting for customers, my master always slept, and it was my duty to watch and offer to passers-by the service of our oars. Those hours, which were often most uncomfortable in the scorching days of summer, were delightful to me under the walls of the Aldini palace, because of a superb female voice, accompanied by a harp, which I could hear distinctly. The window through which those divine sounds came forth was directly over my head, and the protruding balcony served me as a protection against the heat of the sun. That little nook was my Eden, and I never pass the place without a thrill at my heart as I remember those modest joys of my boyhood. A silk curtain shaded the square balcony of white marble, darkened by centuries and covered with convolvulus and climbing plants, carefully tended by the fair hostess of that palatial abode. For she was fair; I had caught a glimpse of her sometimes on the balcony, and I had heard other gondoliers say that she was the most amiable and most courted woman in Venice. I was then hardly sensible of her beauty, although in Venice men of the lower classes have eyes for women of the highest rank, and *vice versa,* so I am told. For my own part, I was all ears; and when she appeared my heart beat fast with joy, because her presence led me to hope that I might soon hear her sing.

I had also heard the gondoliers on that stand say that the instrument with which she accompanied herself was a harp, but their descriptions were so confused that it was impossible for me to form a clear idea of that instrument. Its tones enchanted me, and I was consumed with the longing to see it rather than her. I drew a fanciful picture of it in my mind, for I had been told that it was of pure gold and larger than I was, and my master Masino had seen one decorated with the bust of a beautiful woman who seemed about to fly away, for she had wings. So I saw the harp in my dreams, sometimes in the shape of a siren, sometimes in that of a bird; sometimes I fancied that I saw a beautiful boat decked out with flags pass by, its silk cordage giving forth melodious sounds. Once I dreamed that I found a harp among the reeds and the seaweed; but, just as I put them aside to seize it, I woke with a start and could never remember its shape distinctly.

My curiosity on this subject took such complete possession of my young brain that one day I yielded to a temptation I had conquered many times. While my master was at the wineshop, I climbed on the awning of my gondola, and thence to the sill of a window on the lower floor; then I grasped the balcony rail, drew myself up, climbed over it and found myself behind the curtain.

I had before me the interior of a sumptuously furnished cabinet; but the only object that struck my eye was the harp, standing silent amid the rest of the furniture, above which it towered proudly. The ray of sunlight which shone into the cabinet when I drew the curtain partly aside fell upon the gilding of the instrument, and made the beautiful carved swan that surmounted it gleam brightly. I stood motionless with admiration, never wearying of examining its slightest details, the graceful frame, which reminded me of the prow of a gondola, the slender chords, which seemed to be of spun gold, the gleaming copper, and the satin-lined wooden case, whereon were painted birds, flowers, and butterflies, richly colored and of an exquisite workmanship.

However, amid all those superb objects, the shape and uses of which were quite unfamiliar to me, my mind was still beset by doubt. Was I not mistaken ? Was it really the harp that I was looking at? I determined to make sure of it; I entered the cabinet and placed an awkward, trembling hand on the strings. O rapture ! they answered to my touch. Impelled by indescribable excitement, I made all those resonant voices speak, at random and in a sort of frenzy, and I do not believe that the most skilful and most skilfully led orchestra has ever, since that day, afforded me so much pleasure as the horrible confusion of sounds with which I filled Signora Aldini's apartment.

But my joy was not of long duration. A servant who was at work in the adjoining rooms ran to investigate the noise, and was so enraged to find that a little clodhopper in rags had stolen in in that way and was abandoning himself to the love of art with such shocking disregard of the proprieties, that he set about expelling me by beating me out with his broom. I did not care to be dismissed in that way, and prudently retired to the balcony, intending to go away as I had come. But before I could climb over the balustrade, the servant pounced upon me, and I found myself confronted by the alternative of being beaten or turning a ridiculous somersault. I adopted a violent course, namely, to avoid the blow by stooping quickly, grasping my adversary by the legs, and thus throwing him forward with his breast against the balcony rail. Then to lift him up and throw him into the canal was the affair of a moment. That is the game that the children practise on one another at Chioggia. But I had no time to reflect that the balcony was twenty feet above the water, and that the poor devil of a footman might not know how to swim.

Luckily for him and for me he came to the surface at once and clung to the boats at the *traghetto*. I was horribly frightened when I tossed him over; but, as soon as I saw that he was safe, I began to think about making my escape; for he was roaring with rage and would surely set all the pack of servants in the Aldini Palace upon me. I passed through the first door I saw, and, hurrying through the corridors, was about to go downstairs, when I heard indistinct voices apparently coming toward me. I ran upstairs again in hot haste, and took refuge under the eaves, where I hid in a garret among old worm-eaten pictures and discarded furniture.

I remained there two days and two nights, without a mouthful of food, afraid to venture forth into the midst of my enemies. There were so many people and so much going and coming in that house that one could not take a step without meeting some one. Through the little round windows in the garret I heard the remarks of the servants in the corridors of the floor below. They talked about me almost continuously, indulged in a thousand conjectures concerning my disappearance, and promised to give me a sound thrashing if they succeeded in catching me. I also heard my master on his gondola expressing surprise at my absence, and exulting at the thought of my return, with no less kindly designs. I was brave and strong; but I realized that I should be overborne by numbers. The prospect of being beaten by my master troubled me but little; that was one of the hazards of being an apprentice, which involved no disgrace. But the idea of being chastised by servants was so horrifying to me that I preferred to die of hunger. And my adventure came very near ending in that way. At fifteen years one does not readily endure starvation diet. An old lady's-maid, who came to the garret in search of a runaway pigeon, found instead of her fugitive the poor *barcarolino*, unconscious and almost dead, at the foot of an old canvas representing a Saint Cecilia. The point that impressed me most profoundly in my distress was that the saint had in her arms a harp of antique shape, which I had abundance of leisure to contemplate amid the torments of hunger, and the sight of which became so hateful to me that for a long time thereafter I could not endure the sight or sound of that fatal instrument.

The good creature brought me back to life, and interested Signora Aldini in my fate. I speedily recovered from the effects of my fasting, and my persecutor, appeased by that expiation, accepted my acknowledgment of my wrong-doing, and my somewhat abrupt, but sincere expression of regret. My father, on learning from my master that I had disappeared, had come to Venice. He frowned when Signora Aldini expressed a purpose to take me into her service. He was a rough-mannered man, but proud and independent. In his view it was bad enough that my delicate constitution condemned me to live in the city. I was of too good a family to be a footman, and although gondoliers enjoyed important privileges in private establishments, there was a well-marked distinction in rank between public gondoliers and *gondolieri di casa*. These last were better dressed, to be sure, and shared the comforts of patrician life, but they were ranked as servants, and there was no such blemish in my family. However, Signora Aldini was so gracious and kindly that my excellent father, twisting his red cap about in his hands in his embarrassment, and constantly pulling his pipe from his pocket, as a matter of habit, could find nothing to reply to her affable words and her generous promises. He determined to leave me free to choose, expecting that I would refuse. But I, although I was utterly disgusted with the harp, could think of nothing but music. Signora Aldini exerted a magnetic influence over me which I cannot describe ; it was a genuine passion, but an artistic passion, absolutely platonic and philharmonic. In the small room on the lower floor to which I had been taken —for I had several attacks of fever as a result of my fasting—I could hear her singing, and on those occasions she accompanied herself on the harpsichord, for she played equally well on several instruments. Intoxicated by her voice, I could not even understand my father's scruples, and I accepted without hesitation the post of second gondolier at the Aldini palace.

It was good form in those days to be *well equipped* with gondoliers ; that is to say, that, as the gondola in Venice corresponds to the carriage elsewhere, so gondoliers are at the same time luxuries and necessaries, like horses. All the gondolas being practically alike, according to the sumptuary law of the Republic, which required that they should all be draped in black, persons of wealth could make themselves noticeable among the multitude only by the figures and costumes of their oarsmen. The fashionable patrician's gondola would be propelled, at the stern, by a muscular man, of a masculine type of beauty ; at the bow by a negro dressed in some unusual style, or by a fair-haired native, a sort of page or jockey, clad with taste and elegance, and placed there as an ornament, like the figure-head of a ship.

I was perfectly adapted to that honorable post. I was a genuine child of the lagoons, of fair complexion, ruddy-cheeked, very strong, with a somewhat feminine figure, my head and feet and hands being remarkably small, my chest broad and muscular, my arms and neck white and round and sinewy. Add to this, amber-colored hair, fine and abundant, and naturally curly ; imagine a charming costume, half Figaro and half Cherubino, legs generally bare, sky-blue trunk hose kept up by a scarlet silk sash, and the breast covered simply by a shirt of embroidered linen, whiter than snow ; then you will have an idea of the poor actor in embryo who was called in those days Nello, by contraction of his true name, Daniele Gemello. As it is the fate of small dogs to be petted by idiotic masters and beaten by jealous servants, the ordinary lot of those in my position was a mixture of unbounded tolerance on the part of the former, and of brutal hatred on the part of the latter. Luckily for me, Providence cast my lines in a blessed spot : Bianca Aldini was the incarnation of kindness, indulgence, and charity. Widowed at twenty, she passed her life helping the poor and comforting the afflicted. Where there were tears to be wiped away, or alms to be bestowed, you would soon see her hurrying thither in her gondola, with her little four-year-old daughter in her lap ; a fascinating miniature, so tiny, so pretty, and always so daintily dressed that it seemed as if her mother's lovely hands alone, in all the world, were soft and gentle and tapering enough to touch her without crushing or bruising her. Signora Aldini herself was always dressed with a taste and elegance which all the other ladies in Venice tried in vain to equal ; she was immensely rich, loved luxury, and spent half of her income in the gratification of her artistic tastes and her patrician habits. The other half went in almsgiving, in favors bestowed, in benefactions of every sort. Although that was a sufficiently generous *widow's mite*, as she called it, she artlessly accused herself of lacking energy, of not doing all that she ought ; and, being moved to repentance rather than pride by her charity, she determined every day that she would leave society and devote herself to her own salvation. From this mixture of feminine weakness and Christian virtue you can see that she had not a strong mind, and that her intelligence was no more enlightened than the period and the social circle in which she lived demanded. For all that, I do not know that a better or more delightful woman ever lived. Other women, jealous of her beauty, her wealth and her virtue, avenged themselves by declaring that she was narrow-minded and ignorant. There was some truth in that charge, but Bianca was a most lovable woman, none the less. She had a reserve stock of common sense which prevented her from ever being ridiculous; and as for her lack of education, the ingenuous modesty which resulted from it was an additional charm. I have seen the most enlightened and most serious-minded men gathered about her, never weary of conversing with her.

Living thus at church and at the theatre, in the poor man's garret and at sumptuous palaces, she imposed gratitude or cheerfulness upon one and all. Her disposition was even and playful, and the character of her beauty was enough to shed serenity all about her. She was of medium height, as white as milk, and fresh as a flower; all was gentleness and youth and kindliness. Just as one would have looked in vain for a sharp angle in her own graceful person, so there was never the slightest asperity in her temper, the slightest break in her goodness. As active as the true spirit of devotion, and at the same time as inert as Venetian indolence, she never passed more than two hours during the day in the same place; but in her palace she was always lying on a sofa, and out-of-doors she was always stretched out in her gondola. She said that she was weak on her legs, and she never went up or down stairs without being supported by two persons; in her own apartments she always leaned on the arm of Salomé, a young Jewess, who waited upon her and acted as her companion. People said that Signora Aldini was lame as a result of the fall of a piece of furniture which her husband had pushed upon her in a fit of anger, and which had broken her leg. Although for more than two years she leaned on my arm as she went in and out of her palace, I never discovered the exact truth of the matter, she took so much pains and exerted so much skill to conceal her infirmity.

Despite her benevolence and sweetness of disposition, Bianca lacked neither discrimination nor prudence in the choice of her associates; I can safely say that I have never seen in any other place so many excellent people together. If you detect in me any kindness of heart, any praiseworthy pride, you must attribute it to my stay in that house. It was impossible not to contract the habit there of thinking, speaking and acting rightly; the servants were honest and hardworking, the friends faithful and devoted; even the lovers—for I cannot deny that there were lovers—were loyal and honorable. I had several masters while I was there; of them all the signora was the least imperious. However, they were all kind, or at all events just. Salomé, who was the executive officer of the household, maintained order with some little severity; she seldom smiled, and the great arch of her eyebrows was rarely divided into two quarter circles over her long black eyes. But she had much patience, a keen sense of equity, and a searching glance which never misinterpreted sincerity. Mandola, the chief gondolier and my immediate superior, was a Lombard giant, whose huge black whiskers and muscular frame might have led one to take him for Polyphemus. Nevertheless he was the mildest, calmest and most humane peasant who ever came down from his mountains to the civilization of great cities. Lastly, Count Lanfranchi, the handsomest man in the whole Republic, whom we had to row about every evening in a closed gondola with Signora Aldini, from ten o'clock to midnight, was the most gracious and amiable nobleman whom I have ever met.

I never knew anything of the late Signor Aldini except a full-length portrait, at the entrance to the gallery, in a superb frame, which stood out a little from the wall, and seemed to command a long file of ancestors, each darker and more venerable than the last, who receded, in chronological order, into the obscure depths of that vast room. Torquato Aldini was dressed in the latest fashion of his time, with a shirt-frill of Flanders lace and a morning coat of apple-green cloth with bright red frogs. He was beautifully frizzled and powdered. But, despite the elegance of that pastoral undress, I could not look at him without lowering my eyes; for there was upon his yellowish-brown face, in his blazing black eye, on his sneering and disdainful mouth, in his impassive attitude, and even in the dictatorial gesture of his long, thin, diamond-laden hand, such an expression of overbearing arrogance and inflexible harshness as I had never met with under the roof of that palace. It was a beautiful portrait, and the portrait of a handsome young man. He died at twenty-five, from wounds received in a duel with a Foscari, who dared to say that he was of a better family. He had left behind him a great reputation for courage and decision of character, but it was whispered that he had made his wife very unhappy, and the servants did not seem to regret him. He had kept them in such a state of dread that they never passed that picture after dark, startlingly true to life as it was, without uncovering as they would have done before their former master in person.

His hardness of heart must have caused the signora much suffering, and have disgusted her with the married state, for she refused to enter into a new contract, and rejected the best *partis* in the Republic. And yet she evidently had a yearning for love, for she tolerated Count Lanfranchi's assiduous attentions and seemed to deny him none of the joys of marriage except the indissoluble oath. After a year, the count, abandoning all hope of inspiring in her the necessary confidence for such an engagement as he desired, sought fortune elsewhere, and confessed to her that a certain wealthy heiress gave him more reason to hope. The signora generously gave him his liberty at once. She seemed depressed and ill for a few days, but at the end of a month the Prince of Montalegri took the place in the gondola left vacant by the ungrateful Lanfranchi, and for another year Mandola and I rowed that amiable and seemingly fortunate couple about the lagoons.

I was very deeply attached to the signora. I could imagine nothing on earth lovelier and better than she was. When she turned her sweet, almost motherly glance upon me, when she smilingly said a pleasant word to me—no others could come from her lovely lips— I was so proud and happy that, to afford her a moment's pleasure, I would have thrown myself under the *Bucentaur's* sharp keel. When she gave me an order, I flew; when she leaned on me, my heart beat fast for joy; when, to call the Prince of Montalegri's attention to my fine hair, she gently placed her snow-white hand on my head, I flushed with pride. And yet I was not jealous as I plied my oar with the prince seated beside her. I replied gayly to the kindly jests which the gentlemen of Venice love to exchange with the gondoliers, to test their wit and gift of repartee ; and, despite the extraordinary liberty accorded to the challenged boatman under such circumstances, I had never felt the slightest inclination to make a bitter retort to the prince. He was an excellent young man ; I was grateful to him for consoling the signora for Signor Lanfranchi's desertion. I had not that ridiculous humility which grovels before the privileges of high rank. We hardly recognize those privileges in this country, in the matter of love, and we recognized them even less in those days. There was not so much difference in age between the signora and myself that I might not fall in love with her. The fact is that I should be sorely embarrassed to-day to give a name to my feeling for her at that time. It was love, perhaps, but love as pure as my age ; and tranquil love, because I was neither ambitious nor covetous.

In addition to my youth, my zeal in her service, and my mild and cheerful disposition, my love for music had pleased the signora particularly : it delighted her to see my emotion at the sound of her beautiful voice, and whenever she sang she sent for me. In her affable, unceremonious way, she would bid me come into her cabinet and permit me to sit beside Salomé. It seemed to me that she would have liked to see that inflexible taskmistress lay aside a little of her habitual austerity with me. But Salomé was to me a much more awe-inspiring person than the signora, and I was never tempted to be bold when she was present.

One day the signora asked me if I had any voice. I answered that I used to have, but that I had lost it. She wished me to try it before her. I objected, but she insisted upon it, and I had no choice but to yield. I was in dire distress, and convinced that it would be impossible for me to utter a sound, for it was fully a year since I had thought of such a thing. I was then seventeen years old. My voice had come back, but I had no suspicion of it. I put my head between my hands and tried to remember a passage from the *Jerusalem*. By a mere chance I hit upon the passage which describes Olinde's love for Sophronia, and ends with this line : *Brama assai, poco spera, nulla chiede*. Thereupon, summoning courage, and yelling with all my strength, as if I were in mid-ocean, I made the thunderstruck hangings resound with that plaintive, sonorous lament, to which we sing on the lagoons of the exploits of Roland and the loves of Herminie. I had no suspicion of the effect I should produce. Expecting to hear the hoarse squeak which my throat produced when I last made the experiment, I nearly fell over backward when the organ which I unknowingly concealed within me manifested its power. The pictures hanging on the wall trembled, the signora smiled, and the strings of the harp replied to that resounding voice with a long vibration.

"*Santo Dio!*" cried Salomé, dropping her work and putting her hands over her ears, "the lion of St. Mark's would roar no louder!"

The little Aldini, who was playing on the floor, was so terrified that she began to shriek and weep.

I cannot say what the signora did. I only know that she and the child and Salomé and the harp and the cabinet all disappeared, and that I ran at full speed through the streets, having no idea what demon urged me on, until I reached *Quinta-Valle*. There I jumped into a boat and rowed to the great plain which is now called the Field of Mars, and is still the most deserted spot in the city. As soon as I was alone and free, I began to sing with all the strength of my lungs. Miraculous! 1 had a voice of more power and range than any of the *cupids* I used to admire at Chioggia. Hitherto 1 had supposed that I had not power enough, and I really had too much. It overflowed—it overwhelmed me. I threw myself face downward in the long grass, and, yielding to a paroxysm of delirious joy, burst into tears. O the first tears of the artist! They only can be compared in sweetness, or in bitterness, with the first tears of the lover.

Then I began to sing again, and repeated a hundred times in succession the scattered fragments I had remembered. As I sang on, the ear-splitting harshness of my voice wore off, and I felt that it became more flexible and tractable every moment. I felt no fatigue, the more I practised, the easier my respiration seemed. Then I ventured to try some of the operatic arias and romanzas which I had heard the signora sing in the past two years. In those two years I had worked hard and learned a great deal without suspecting it. Method had found its way into my head, by virtue and by instinct, and musical feeling into my heart by intuition and sympathy. I have very great respect for study, but I must admit that no singer ever studied less than myself. I was blessed with a marvellous readiness and memory. If I had once heard a passage, I could repeat it instantly and accurately. I tried that experiment that very day, and succeeded in singing from beginning to end the most difficult pieces in Signora Aldini's repertory.

The approach of night warned me to allow my excitement to subside. Then for the first time I realized that I had absented myself from my duties for a whole day, and I returned to the palace, embarrassed and repenting bitterly of my fault. It was the first of that sort I had committed, and I dreaded nothing so much as a rebuke from the signora, however mild it might be. She was at supper, and I crept timidly behind her chair. I never waited on her at table, for I had retained the pride of a true Chioggian, and had surrendered none of the exemptions attached to my privileged post. But, seeking to repair my fault by an act of humility, I took from Salomé's hands the porcelain dish she was about to offer her, and put out my hand awkwardly enough. Signora Aldini pretended at first not to notice, and allowed me to serve her thus for several minutes; then, as she stealthily looked up and met my piteous glance, she suddenly burst out laughing, and threw herself back in her chair.

"Your ladyship is spoiling him," said the stern Salomé, repressing an imperceptible desire to share her mistress's merriment.

"Why should I scold him?" replied the signora. "He frightened himself this morning, and ran away to punish himself, poor boy! I will bet that he has eaten nothing to-day. Go to your supper, Nellino. I forgive you on condition that you will sing no more."

This kindly sarcasm seemed very bitter to me. It was the first one I had ever noticed; for, despite all the opportunities offered for the development of my vanity, that was a sentiment with which I was not as yet acquainted. But pride awoke in me with power, and by making sport of my voice, she seemed to deny my heart and to attack my very life.

From that day the lessons which the signora unconsciously gave me, by practising in my presence, became more and more profitable to me. Every evening, as soon as my duties were at an end, I went to the Field of Mars to practise, and I knew that I was making progress. Soon the signora's lessons were no longer sufficient for me. She sang for her own pleasure, displaying a superb indifference for study, and making no effort to perfect herself. I had a most immoderate longing to go to the theatre; but, during the whole time of the performance, it was my lot to watch the gondola, as Mandola enjoyed the privilege of taking a seat in the pit or listening in the corridors. At last, however, I induced him to let me take his place during a single act of the opera at La Fenice. The opera was the *Secret Marriage*. I will not attempt to describe my feelings: I nearly went mad, and, breaking the promise I had made my companion, I allowed him to cool his heels in the gondola, and never thought of going out until I found that the hall was empty and in darkness.

After that I felt an irresistible, imperious craving to go to the theatre every night. I dared not ask Signora Aldini's permission; I was afraid that she would again make fun of my unfortunate passion—as she called it—for music. However, I must go to La Fenice or die. I had the reprehensible thought of leaving the signora's service and earning my living as a *facchino* during the day, so that I might have both time and means to go to the theatre. I calculated that with the small sum I had saved at the Aldini Palace, and by reducing my expenditure for food and clothing to what was absolutely necessary, I might be able to gratify my passion. I also thought of entering the employ of the theatre as a scene-shifter, supernumerary, or lamp-lighter; the most humble post would have seemed delightful to me, provided that I could listen to music every day. At last I determined to open my heart to the good-humored Montalegri. He had heard of my musical misadventure. He began by laughing; then, as I boldly persisted, he demanded, as a condition of his assistance, that I should let him hear my voice. I hesitated a long while; I was afraid that he would discourage me by his jests, and although I had no definite plans for the future, I felt that to deprive me of the hope of being able to sing some day would be like tearing out my life. However, I submitted to the inevitable : I sang in a trembling voice a fragment of one of the airs which I had heard a single time at the theatre. My emotion won the prince's heart; I saw in his eyes that he took pleasure in listening to me; I took courage and sang better and better. He raised his hands two or three times to applaud, but checked himself for fear of interrupting me ; then I sang really well, and when I had finished, the prince, who was a genuine dilettante, almost kissed me, and praised me in the warmest terms. He took me to the signora and presented my petition, which was granted on the spot. But she too wanted me to sing, and I would not consent. My proud persistence in refusing astonished Signora Aldini without irritating her. She thought that she would overcome it later, but she did not easily succeed. The more I attended the theatre, and the more I practised and improved, the more conscious I became of all that I still lacked, and the more I dreaded to allow others to hear me and judge me before I was sure of myself. At last one superb moonlight night, on the Lido, as the signora, by lengthening her usual row, had made me miss the theatre and my hour of solitary practice, I was suddenly seized with a longing to sing, and I yielded to the inspiration. The signora and her lover listened to me in silence ; and, when I had finished, they did not address a word to me, either of praise or blame. Mandola alone, having the keen taste for music of a true Lombard, cried several times when he heard my youthful tenor: "*Corpo del diavolo! che buon basso!*"

I was a little hurt by my mistress's heedlessness or indifference. I knew that I had sung well enough to deserve a word of praise from her mouth. Nor did I understand the prince's coldness after the praise he had lavished on me two months earlier. I learned afterward that my mistress was amazed by my talent and my powers, but that she had determined to seem unmoved by my first attempt, to punish me for making her beg so long.

I took the lesson to heart, and a few days later, when she called on me to sing while she was in the gondola, I complied with a good grace. She was alone, lying on the cushions of the gondola, and seemed to be in a melancholy frame of mind, which was by no means usual with her. She did not speak a word to me during the row; but when we returned and I offered my arm to assist her up the steps of the palace, she said these words to me, which left me in a strangely excited state:

"Nello, you have done me a vast deal of good. I thank you."

On the days following, I myself offered to sing. She seemed to accept my offer with gratitude. The heat was most intense and the theatres were closed; the signora said that she was ill; but what made the most impression on me was the fact that the prince, who was usually so assiduous in his attendance, had ceased to come with her oftener than once in two or three or even four evenings, I thought that he too was beginning to be unfaithful and I grieved for my poor mistress. I could not understand her obstinacy in refusing to marry; it seemed most unfair to me that Montalegri, who seemed to be so kind and gentle, should be sacrificed to the sins of the late Torquato Aldini. On the other hand, I could not understand why so sweet and lovely a woman should have for lovers only base speculators who were more covetous of her fortune than attached to her person, and sickened of the latter as soon as they despaired of obtaining the former.

These thoughts engrossed me so completely for several

days that, notwithstanding my profound respect for my mistress, I could not refrain from communicating my ideas to Mandola.

"Don't make that mistake," he replied; "what has happened this time is just the opposite of what happened with Lanfranchi. The signora is sick of the prince and invents every day some new excuse to prevent his coming with her. What is the reason? That I cannot guess, for we see her all the time and know that she is alone, that she has no rendezvous with anyone. Perhaps she is turning religious altogether, and means to cut loose from society."

That same evening I started to sing to the signora a hymn to the Virgin; but she interrupted me instantly, saying that she had no desire to sleep, and asked for the loves of Armide and Renaud.

"He made a mistake," said Mandola, who had a certain shrewdness of his own, pretending to apologize for me. I changed my selection, and was listened to with attention.

I soon discovered that by singing in the open air and while the gondola was in motion, I tired myself a good deal, and that my voice was suffering. I consulted a teacher of music who came to the palace to give lessons to little Alezia Aldini, then six years old. He told me that, if I continued to sing out-of-doors, I should ruin my voice before the end of the year. That threat frightened me so that I resolved to sing no more under those conditions. But on the next day the signora asked me, with such a melancholy air, with such a sweet glance and such pale cheeks, to sing the barcarole from *La Biondina,* that I had not the heart to deny her the only pleasure that she had seemed capable of enjoying for some time past.

It was evident that she was growing thin and losing her bloom; she kept the prince more and more at a distance. She passed her life in the gondola, and even neglected the poor a little. She seemed to be giving way to a profound depression the cause of which we sought in vain.

There was one week when she apparently tried to divert her thoughts. She surrounded herself with company, and in the evening her gondola was attended by several others in which she placed her friends and the musicians hired to sing for them. Once she asked me to sing. I declined, alleging my unfitness to perform in the presence of professional musicians and numerous *dilettanti*. She insisted, gently at first, then with some irritation; I continued to refuse, and at last she ordered me, in a most imperative tone, to obey her. It was the first time in her life that she had lost her temper. And I, instead of reflecting that it was her illness which had changed her disposition thus, and humoring her, yielded to the suggestion of invincible pride, and declared that I was not her slave, that I had hired myself to her to row her gondola and not to entertain her guests; and, in a word, that I had nearly ruined my voice for her amusement, and that she rewarded me so ill for my self-sacrifice that I would sing no more for her or anyone else. She made no reply; the friends who accompanied her, amazed at my audacity, held their peace. A few minutes later, Salomé uttered a sharp exclamation and seized little Alezia, who, having fallen asleep in her mother's arms, nearly fell into the water. The signora had fainted some moments before, and no one had noticed it.

I dropped my oar; I talked at random; I went to the signora's side; I should have done some insane thing or other, if the prudent Salomé had not imperiously sent me back to my post. The signora came to herself and we made haste back to the palace. But the company was surprised and shocked, the music was all awry; and, for my own part, I was in such despair and terror, that my trembling hands could not hold the oar. I lost my wits, I ran into all the other gondolas. Mandola swore at me; but I, deaf to his warnings, turned every moment to look at Signora Aldini, whose pale face seemed, in the moonlight, to bear the stamp of death.

She passed a bad night; the next day she was feverish and kept her bed. Salomé refused to admit me. In spite of her refusal I stole into the bedroom and dropped on my knees beside the signora, weeping bitterly. She held out her hand, which I covered with kisses, and told me that I had done right to resist her.

"I have been exacting, capricious and cruel for some time past," she added with an angelic sweetness. "You must forgive me, Nello; I am ill, and I feel that I cannot control my temper as usual. I forget that you are not destined to remain a gondolier, and that a brilliant future is in store for you. Forgive me for this too; my friendship for you is so great that I had a selfish desire to keep you with me, and to bury your talent in this humble and obscure position which is ruining your prospects. You defended your independence and your dignity and you did well. Henceforth you shall be free, you shall study music; I will spare no pains to keep your voice unharmed and to develop your talent; you shall perform no other service for me than such as is dictated by affection and gratitude."

I swore that I would serve her all my life; that I would rather die than leave her; and, in truth, my attachment to her was so deep and so pure that I did not consider that I was taking a rash oath.

She was better after that, and insisted on my taking

my first lessons in singing. She was present, and seemed to take the keenest interest. In the intervals between the lessons, she made me study and recite to her the elementary principles of music, of which I had not the slightest idea, although I had instinctively conformed to them when I sang naturally.

My progress was rapid. I ceased to do hard work of any kind. The signora pretended that the double movement caused by the two oars in alternation tired her, and Mandola's wages were doubled so that he might not complain of having to do all the work alone. As for myself, I was always in the gondola, but I sat in the bow, occupied solely in looking into my mistress's eyes to divine what I should do to please her. Her lovely eyes were very sad—very pensive. Her health improved at times, then became worse again. That was my only sorrow, but it was very keen.

She lost her strength more and more, and the assistance of our arms was no longer sufficient when she went up-stairs. It became Mandola's duty to carry her like a child, as I carried little Alezia. That young lady grew more beautiful every day; but her style of beauty and her temperament made her the exact opposite of her mother. Alezia was as dark as her mother was fair. Her hair already fell to her knees in two heavy ebony braids; her little, soft, round arms stood forth like those of a young Moor against her silk clothing, always white as snow; for she was consecrated to the Virgin. As for her temperament, it was very strange for one of her years. I have never seen a child so grave and distrustful and silent. She seemed to have inherited the haughty nature of Signor Torquato. She was never on familiar terms with anyone; she never used the familar words of address with any of us. A caress from Salomé she seemed to consider an insult, and the very utmost I could obtain, by dint of carrying her, waiting upon her and flattering her, was permission to kiss once a week the tips of her little pink fingers, of which she was already as careful as the most coquettish woman could have been. She was very cold to her mother, and passed long hours seated by her side in the gondola, with her eyes fixed on the water, silent, apparently insensible to everything, and as dreamy as a statue. But if the signora ventured to reprove her ever so mildly, or if she went to bed because of an attack of fever, the little one would fly into one of those paroxysms of frantic despair which aroused fears for her life or her reason.

One day she fainted in my arms because Mandola, who was carrying her mother, slipped on one of the steps and fell with her. The signora was slightly hurt, and from that day was unwilling to trust the skill of the Lombard giant. She asked me if I were strong enough to take his place. I was then at the height of my muscular development, and I told her that I could carry four women like herself and eight children like hers. After that I always carried her, for her strength did not return up to the time that I left her.

The time soon came when the signora seemed to be less light and the staircase harder to ascend. It was not because her weight was increasing, but because my strength failed me as soon as I took her in my arms. At first I did not understand it; then I reproached myself bitterly; but my emotion was insurmountable. That willowy and voluptuous figure which abandoned itself to me, that charming face almost touching mine, that alabaster arm around my bare and burning neck, that perfumed hair mingling with mine—it was too much for a lad of seventeen. It was impossible for her not to feel the hurried beating of my heart, and read in my eyes the disturbance that she caused in my senses. "I tire you," she would sometimes say with a languishing air. I could not reply to that sarcasm; my head would begin to whirl, and I was forced to run away as soon as I had placed her in her chair. One day it happened that Salomé was not, as usual, in her cabinet to receive her. I had some difficulty in arranging the cushions so that she could sit comfortably. My arms met around her waist. I found myself at her feet, my dizzy head resting on her knees. She ran her fingers through my hair. The sudden quivering of that hand revealed to me that of which I had had no conception. I was not the only one who was moved; I was not the only one on the point of giving way. We were no longer servant and mistress, gondolier and signora; we were a young man and a young woman who loved each other. A sudden light flashed through my mind and darted from my eyes. She hastily pushed me away, and exclaimed, in a stifled voice: "*Go!*" I obeyed, but as a conqueror. I was no longer the servant receiving an order, but the lover making a sacrifice.

Thereupon blind desire took possession of my whole being. I did not reflect; I felt neither fear nor scruple nor doubt. I had but one fixed idea, to be alone with Bianca. But that was more difficult than one might presume from her independent position. It seemed as if Salomé divined the danger, and had taken upon herself the task of protecting her mistress from it. She never left her, except sometimes at night when little Alezia wanted to go to bed at the hour when her mother went out in the gondola. At such times Mandola inevitably accompanied us on the lagoons. I saw plainly enough, by the signora's expression and her uneasiness, that she could not help desiring a tête-à-tête with me; but she was too weak either to seek it or to avoid it. I did not lack boldness or resolution, but not for anything under heaven would I have compromised her; and furthermore, so long as I had not actually won a victory in that delicate condition of affairs, my rôle might well be supremely ridiculous, even contemptible, in the eyes of the signora's other servants.

Luckily honest Mandola, who was not devoid of penetration, had for me an affection which never wavered. I should not be surprised, although he never gave me the right to assert it, if love had sometimes made a soft heart beat fast beneath that rough bark, when he carried the signora in his arms. It was extremely imprudent for a young woman to betray the secret of her love-affairs to two young men of our age, and almost flaunt them in our faces; and it was impossible for us to be witnesses of the good fortune of other men, for two years, without being unduly tempted. However that may be, I find it difficult to believe that Mandola would have detected so readily what was taking place in my heart, if something of the same sort had not taken place in his. One evening, as I sat at the bow of the gondola, lost in thought, my face hidden in my hands, waiting for the signora to send for us, he said to me: *"Nello! Nello!!!"*—nothing more, but in a tone which seemed to me to mean so much that I raised my head and looked at him with a sort of terror, as if my fate were in his hands.—He stifled something like a sigh, as he added the popular saying: *"Sara quel che sara!"*

"What do you mean?" I cried, rising and grasping his arm.

"Nello! Nello!" he repeated, shaking his head. At

that moment they came to tell me to go up and bring the signora to the gondola; but Mandola's meaning glance followed me up the steps and moved me strangely.

That same day Mandola applied to Signora Aldini for a week's leave of absence, to go and see his sick father. Bianca seemed surprised and dismayed by the request; but she granted it at once, adding: "But who will row my gondola?"—"Nello," Mandola replied, watching me closely. "But he cannot row alone," rejoined the signora. "No matter, take me home, to-morrow we will look for a temporary substitute. Go to see your father, and take good care of him; I will pray for him."

The next day the signora sent for me, and asked me if I had made inquiries for a gondolier. I replied only by an audacious smile. The signora turned pale and said to me in a trembling voice: "You will attend to it to-morrow; I shall not go out to-day."

I realized my mistake; but the signora had shown more fear than anger, and my hope augmented my insolence. Toward evening I went and asked her if I should bring the gondola to the steps. She replied coldly: "I told you this morning that I should not go out." I did not lose courage. "The weather has changed, signora," I said, "the wind is as warm as the sirocco. It is fine weather for you to-night." She bestowed a withering glance upon me, saying: "I didn't ask you what the weather is. How long has it been your place to advise me?" The battle was on, I did not retreat. "Since you have seemed disposed to allow yourself to die," I replied vehemently. She seemed to yield to some magnetic force; for she languidly dropped her head on her hand, and in a faint voice bade me bring the gondola.

I carried her down to it. Salomé attempted to accompany her. I took it upon myself to say to her in an imperative tone that her mistress ordered her to remain with Signora Alezia. I saw the blood come and go in the signora's cheeks as I took the oar and eagerly pushed against the marble steps which seemed to flee behind us. When I was a few rods from the palace, it seemed to me that I had conquered the world, and that my victory was assured, all inconvenient witnesses being out of the way. I rowed furiously out into the middle of the lagoons, without turning my head, without speaking a word, without stopping for breath. I had the appearance of a lover carrying off his mistress much more than of a gondolier rowing his employer. When we were quite alone, I dropped my oar and let the boat drift; but at that point all my courage abandoned me; it was impossible for me to speak to the signora, I dared not even look at her. She gave me no encouragement, and I rowed her back to the palace, mortified enough to have resumed the trade of boatman without obtaining the reward I hoped for.

Salomé showed some temper with me, and humiliated me several times, accusing me of having a surly and preoccupied air. I could never say a word to the signora without a rebuke from the maid, who always declared that I did not express myself respectfully. The signora, who usually defended me, did not even seem to notice the mortifications to which I was subjected that evening. I was incensed beyond words. For the first time I was really ashamed of my position, and I should have thought seriously of quitting it, if the irresistible magnet of desire had not kept me in bondage.

For several days I suffered tortures. The signora pitilessly allowed me to exhaust my strength rowing her about at midday, in the dry, intensely hot, autumn weather, before the eyes of the whole city, who had seen me for a long time previously seated in her gondola, at her feet, almost at her side, and who saw me now, dripping with perspiration, fallen from the sublime profession of troubadour to the laborious trade of gondolier. My love changed to wrath. Two or three times I felt a shameful temptation to treat her disrespectfully in public; then I was ashamed of myself and my dejection became the more complete.

One morning, the fancy seized her to go ashore on the Lido. The shore was deserted, the sand sparkled in the sunlight; my head was burning hot, the perspiration was running down my breast in streams. As I stooped to lift Signora Aldini, she passed her silk handkerchief over my dripping forehead, and gazed at me with a sort of loving compassion.

"*Poveretto!*" she said, "you are not made for the trade to which I condemn you!"

"I would go to the galleys for you," I replied hotly.

"And sacrifice your beautiful voice," she rejoined, "and the great talent you may acquire, and the noble profession of musical artist to which you may attain?"

"Everything!" I replied, dropping on my knees before her.

"You do not mean it!" she retorted, with a melancholy air. "Return to your place," she added, pointing to the bow. "I wish to rest a while here."

I returned to the bow, but I left the door of the *camerino* open. I could see her lying on the black cushions, fair and pale, wrapped in her black cape, buried and, as it were hidden in the black velvet of that mysterious bower, which seems made for stealthy pleasures and forbidden joys. She resembled a beautiful swan which swims into a dark grotto to avoid the hunter. I felt that my reason was abandoning me; I crept to her side and fell on my knees. To give her a kiss and then die in expiation of my crime was my whole thought. Her eyes were closed, she pretended to be asleep, but she felt the fire of my breath. Then she called to me aloud, as if she believed me to be at a distance, and pretended to wake gradually, to give me time to go away. She bade me go to the *bottega* on the Lido to fetch her some lemonade, then closed her eyes again. I put one foot on shore, and that was all. I stepped back into the gondola and stood still, gazing at her. She opened her eyes, and her glance seemed to draw me to her by a thousand chains of steel and diamond. I took one step toward her, she closed her eyes again; I took another step, and she opened them, assuming an expression of contemptuous surprise. I went ashore again, then returned to the gondola. This cruel game lasted several minutes. She attracted and spurned me as the hawk plays with the mortally wounded sparrow. Anger took possession of me; I slammed the door of the *camerino* so violently that the glass was shivered. She uttered a cry which I did not deign to notice, but rushed ashore, singing in a voice of thunder, which I thought reckless and devil-may-care:

> "La Biondina in gondoleta
> L'altra sera mi o mena;
> Dal piazer la povareta
> La x' a in boto adormenta.
> E la dormiva su sto bracio
> Me intanto la svegliava;
> E la barca che ninava
> La tornava a adormenzar."

I sat down upon one of the Jewish tombstones on the Lido, and remained there a long while; I purposely compelled her to wait for me. Then, of a sudden, thinking that she might be suffering with thirst, I ran, stricken with remorse, to fetch the drink for which she had asked me, and carried it to her with deep solicitude. And yet I hoped that she would reprimand me; I would have liked to be dismissed from my employment, for it had become intolerable to me. She received me with no trace of anger; indeed she thanked me sweetly as she took the glass I handed her. Thereupon I saw that her hand was bleeding, it had been cut by the broken glass. I could not restrain my tears. I saw that hers were flowing too; but she did not speak to me, and I dared not break that silence, fraught with loving reproaches and timid passion.

I determined to stamp out my insane love and to leave Venice. I tried to persuade myself that the signora had never returned it, and that I had flattered myself with an impertinent hope; but every moment her glance, her tone of voice, her gesture, even her sadness, which seemed to increase and decrease with mine, all combined to revive my insane confidence and to lead me to dangerous dreams.

Fate seemed determined to deprive us of what little strength we still retained. Mandola did not return. I was a very indifferent oarsman, despite my zeal and strength; I was not familiar with the lagoons, I had always been so absorbed by my own thoughts as I went in and out among them! One evening I went astray in the salt marshes that stretch from the St. George canal to the Marana canal. The rising tide covered those vast plains of sand and sea-weed; but it began to fall again before I succeeded in rowing back into clear water; I could see the tops of the aquatic plants moving in the breeze amid the foam. I pulled hard, but in vain. The ebb tide laid bare a vast expanse of marsh, and the gondola stranded gently on a bed of seaweed and shells. Night had spread its veil over the sky and the waters, the sea-birds lighted all around us, by thousands, filling the air with their plaintive cries. I called for a long time, but my voice was lost in space; no fishing vessel chanced to be at anchor near the marsh, no craft of any sort approached us. We must needs resign ourselves to the necessity of awaiting some chance succor or the next morning's tide. This last alternative was exceedingly disquieting; I dreaded the cold night air for my mistress's sake, and above all, the unhealthy vapors that rise from the marshes at daybreak; I tried in vain to pull the gondola to a pool of water. Aside from the fact that we should simply have gained a very few feet, it would have taken more than six men to raise the boat from the bed she had made for herself. Thereupon I determined to wade through the swamp, up to my waist in mud, until I reached the channel, and to swim across in quest of help. It was an insane undertaking; for I did not know the lay of the land, and where the fishermen adroitly walk about to gather *sea-fruit*, I should have been lost in bogs and quick-sands after a very few steps. When the signora saw that I was inclined to resist her prohibition, and was about to take the risk, she sprang to her feet, and, mustering strength to remain in that position for an instant, she threw her arms about me and fell back, almost pressing me to her heart. Thereupon I forgot all my anxiety, and cried frantically:

"Yes! yes! let us stay here; let us never leave this spot; let us die here of joy and love, and may the Adriatic not wake to-morrow to rescue us!"

In the first moment of emotion she was very near abandoning herself to my transports; but she soon recovered the strength with which she had armed herself.

"Well, yes," she said, kissing me on the forehead; "yes, I love you, and I have loved you for a long while. It was because I loved you that I refused to marry Lanfranchi, for I could not make up my mind to place an everlasting obstacle between you and me. It was because I loved you that I endured Montalegri's love, fearing that I might succumb to my passion for you, and being determined to combat it; it was because I loved you that I sent him away, being unable to endure longer that love which I did not share; it is because I love you that I am still determined not to give way to what I feel to-day; for I propose to give you proofs of a veritable love, and I owe to your pride, so long humbled, some other recompense than vain caresses, another title than that of lover."

I did not understand that language. What other title than that of lover could I desire, what greater happiness than that of possessing such a mistress? I had had some absurd moments of pride and frenzy, but at that time I was unhappy, I did not think that she loved me.

"So long as you do love me," I cried; "so long as you tell me so as you do now, in the mystery of darkness, and every evening, out of sight of the curious and envious, give me a kiss as you did just now; so long as you are mine in secret, in God's bosom, shall I not be prouder and happier than the Doge of Venice? What more do I need than to live beside you and to know that you belong to me? Ah! let all the world remain in ignorance of it; I do not need to make others jealous in order to be happy beyond words, and the opinion of other people is not necessary to the pride and joy of my heart."

"And yet," replied Bianca, "it will humiliate you to be my servant after this, will it not?"

"I was humiliated this morning," I cried; "to-morrow I shall be proud of it."

"What!" she said, "would you not despise me if, after abandoning myself to your love, I should leave you in a state of degradation?"

"There can be no degradation in serving one who loves me," I replied. "If you were my wife, do you think that I would allow anybody but myself to carry you? Could I think of anything except taking care of you and amusing you? Salomé is not humiliated to be in your service, and yet you do not love her as much as you love me, *signora mia*?"

"O my noble-hearted boy!" cried Bianca, pressing my head against her breast with deep emotion; "O pure and unselfish soul! Who will dare now to say that there are no great hearts save those that are born in palaces! Who will dare deny the honor and saintliness of these plebeian natures, ranked so low by our hateful prejudices and our absurd disdain! You are the only man who ever loved me for myself alone, the only man whose aim was not my rank or my fortune!—Very well! you shall share them both, you shall make me forget the miseries of my first marriage, and replace with your rustic name the hateful name of Aldini, which I bear with regret! You shall command my vassals and be at once the lord of my estates and the master of my life. Nello, will you marry me?"

If the earth had opened under my feet, or if the skies had fallen on my head, I could not have experienced a more violent shock of amazement than that which struck me dumb in the face of such a question. When I had recovered somewhat from my stupefaction, I do not know what reply I made, for my head was going round, and it was impossible for me to think coherently. All that my natural good sense could do was to put aside honors too heavy for my age and my inexperience. Bianca insisted.

"Listen," she said; "I am not happy. My cheerfulness has long been a cloak for intense suffering, until now, as you see, I am ill and can no longer conceal my ennui. My position in society is false and very distasteful to me ; my position in my own esteem is worse still, and God is dissatisfied with me. You know that I am not of patrician descent. Torquato Aldini married me on account of the great fortune my father had amassed in business. That haughty nobleman never saw in me anything more than the instrument of his fortune, he never deigned to treat me as his equal ; some of his relatives encouraged him in maintaining the absurd and cruel attitude of lord and master which he assumed toward me at the outset ; others blamed him severely for having contracted a misalliance in order to pay his debts, and treated him coldly after his marriage. After his death they all refused to see me, and I found myself without any family ; for by entering the family of a noble I had forfeited the esteem and affection of my own people. I had married Torquato for love, and those of my relatives who did not consider me insane believed me to be guided by foolish vanity and vile ambition. That is why, despite my wealth and my youth and an obliging and inoffensive disposition, you see my salons almost empty and my social circle so restricted. I have some warm friends, and their company satisfies my heart. But I am entirely unfamiliar with the intoxication of society at large, and it has not treated me so well that I am called upon to sacrifice my happiness to it. I know that by marrying you I shall draw down upon myself not its indifference simply but its irrevocable malediction. Do not be alarmed ; you see that it is a very trifling sacrifice on my part."

"But why marry me ? " said I. " Why invite that malediction to no purpose ? for I do not need your fortune to be happy, nor do you need a solemn contract on my part to be sure that I shall love you forever."

" Whether you are my husband or my lover," Bianca

replied, "the world will find it out all the same, and I shall be cursed and despised none the less. Since your love must necessarily, in one way or the other, separate me altogether from society, I desire at least to be reconciled to God, and to find in this love of mine, sanctified by the Church, the strength to despise society as it despises me. I have lived in sin for a long while, I have sinned without adding to my happiness, I have risked my salvation and have not found gladness of heart. Now I have found it and I wish to enjoy it, stainless and cloudless; I wish to sleep, free from remorse, on the bosom of the man I love; I wish to be able to say to the world: 'It is you who destroy and corrupt hearts. Nello's love has saved and purified me, and I have a refuge against you ; God permitted me to love Nello, and bids me love him until death.'"

Bianca talked to me a long while in this strain. There was weakness, childishness and pure goodness in these ingenuous plottings of her pride, her love and her piety. I was not very strong myself. It was not long since I had been accustomed to kneel, night and morning, on my father's boat, before the image of St. Anthony painted on the sail; and although the beautiful women of Venice diverted my thoughts sadly in the basilica, I never missed attending mass, and I still had on my neck the scapulary my mother hung there as she gave me her blessing on the day I left Chioggia. So I allowed Signora Aldini to triumph over my scruples and persuade me ; and without further resistance or promises, I passed the night at her feet, as submissive as a child to her religious scruples, intoxicated with the pleasure of simply kissing her hand and inhaling the perfume of her fan. It was a lovely night. The twinkling stars trembled in the little pools which the tide had left on the marsh ; the breeze murmured in the green grasses. From time to time we saw in the distance the light of a gondola gliding over the waves, but it did not occur to us to call for help. The voice of the Adriatic breaking on the farther shore of the Lido reached our ears, monotonous and majestic. We indulged in countless enchanting dreams; we formed countless deliciously trivial plans. The moon sank slowly and was shrouded in the dark waves on the horizon, like a chaste virgin in her winding-sheet. We were as chaste as she, and she seemed to glance at us with a friendly expression before plunging into the sea.

But soon the cold made itself felt, and a sheet of white mist spread over the marsh. I closed the *camerino* and wrapped Bianca in my red cape. I sat down beside her, put my arms about her to shelter her, and warmed her arms and hands with my breath. A delicious calm seemed to have descended upon her heart since she had almost extorted from me a promise to marry her. She rested her head lightly on my shoulder. The night was far advanced; for more than six hours we had poured forth the ardent love of our hearts in tender and impassioned words. A pleasant sensation of weariness stole over me as well, and we fell asleep in each other's arms, as pure as the dawn that was beginning to appear on the horizon. It was our wedding-night—our only night of love; a spotless night, which was never repeated, and its memory never marred.

Loud voices woke me. I ran to the bow of the gondola and saw several men approaching us. At the usual time of starting out to fish, a family of fishermen had discovered the stranded craft, and they assisted me to drag her to the Marana Canal, whence I rowed rapidly to the palace.

How happy I was as I placed my foot on the first step!

I thought no more of the palace than of Bianca's fortune; but I had her in my arms who thenceforth was my property, my life, my mistress in the noble and blessed sense of the word! But my joy ended there. Salomé appeared in the doorway of that terror-stricken house, where no one had closed an eye during the night. Salomé was pale, and it was evident that she had been weeping; it was probably the only time in her life. She did not venture to question her mistress: perhaps she had already read upon my brow the reason why the night had seemed so short to me. It had been long enough to all the occupants of the palace. They all believed that some horrible accident had befallen their dear mistress. A number of them had wandered about all night, looking for us; others had passed the time in prayer, burning little tapers before the image of the Virgin. When their anxiety was allayed and their curiosity gratified, I noticed that their thoughts took another direction and their faces a different expression. They scrutinized my face—the women especially—with insulting eagerness. As for Salomé's expression, it was so withering that I could not endure it. Mandola arrived from the country in the midst of the commotion. He understood in an instant what was going on, and, putting his mouth to my ear, begged me to be prudent. I pretended not to know what he meant; I did my best to submit with an air of innocence to the investigations of the others. But in a few moments I was unable to endure my anxiety, and I went into Bianca's room.

I found her weeping bitterly beside her daughter's bed. The child had been awakened in the middle of the night by the noise of the constant going and coming of the frightened servants. She had listened to their comments on the signora's prolonged absence, and, believing that her mother was drowned, she had gone into convulsions. She had barely become calm when I entered, and Bianca was blaming herself for the child's suffering, as if she had wilfully caused it.

"O my Bianca," I said to her, "be comforted and rejoice because your child and all those about you love you so passionately. I will love you even more than they do, so that you may be the happiest of women."

"Do not say that the others love me," she replied with some bitterness. "It seems to me that under their breaths they are calling this love of mine, which they have already divined, a crime. Their glances are insulting to me, their words wound me, and I greatly fear that they have let slip some imprudent remark in my daughter's hearing. Salomé is openly impertinent to me this morning. It is high time for me to put an end to these insolent comments on my conduct. You see, Nello, they look upon my loving you as a crime, and they approved of my supposed love for the avaricious Lanfranchi. They are all low-minded or foolish creatures. I must inform them this very day that I passed the night, not with my lover, but with my husband. It is the only way to make them respect you and refrain from betraying me."

I dissuaded her from acting so hastily. I reminded her that she might perhaps repent; that she had not reflected sufficiently; that I myself needed time to consider her offer seriously; and that she had not sufficiently weighed the consequences of her decision, with respect to its possible future effect upon her daughter. I obtained her promise to be patient and to act prudently.

It was impossible for me to form an enlightened judgment regarding my situation. It was intoxicating, and I was a mere boy. Nevertheless, a sort of instinctive repugnance warned me to distrust the fascinations of love and fortune. I was excited, anxious, torn between desire and fear. In the brilliant destiny that was offered me, I saw but one thing—possession of the woman I loved. All the wealth by which she was surrounded was not even an accessory to my happiness, it was a disagreeable condition for me in my heedlessness to accept. I was like one who has never suffered and can conceive of no better or worse state than that in which he has always lived. In the Aldini Palace I was free and happy. Petted by all alike, permitted to gratify all my whims, I had no responsibility, nothing to fatigue my body or my mind. Singing, sleeping, and boating, that was substantially the whole of my life, and you Venetians who are listening to me know whether any life is sweeter or better adapted to our indolent and careless natures. I imagined the rôle of husband and master as something analogous to the superintendence exercised by Salomé over household affairs, and such a rôle was very far from flattering my ambition. That palace, of which I had the freedom, was my property in the pleasantest sense of the word : I enjoyed all its pleasures without any of its cares. Let my mistress add the joys of love, and I should be the King of Italy.

Another thing that disheartened me was Salomé's gloomy air and the embarrassed, mysterious and suspicious demeanor of the other servants. There were many of them, and they were all excellent people, who had treated me hitherto as a child of the family. In that silent reprobation which I felt hovering over me, there was a warning which I could not, which I did not wish to disdain ; for, while it was due in some measure to a natural feeling of jealousy, it was dictated even more by the affectionate interest which the signora inspired.

What would I not have given in those moments of dire

perplexity to have a judicious adviser? But I did not know whom to apply to, and I was the sole confidant of my mistress's secrets. She passed the day in bed with her daughter, and sent for me the next day, to repeat to me all that she had said on the marsh. All the time that she was speaking to me, it seemed to me that she was right, and that she had a triumphant answer to all my scruples; but when I was alone again, my distress and irresolution returned.

I went up into the gallery and threw myself upon a chair. My eyes wandered absent-mindedly from one to another of that long line of ancestors whose portraits formed the only heritage that Torquato Aldini had been able to bequeath to his daughter. Their smoke-begrimed faces, their beards, cut square, and pointed, and diamond-shaped, their black velvet robes and ermine-lined cloaks, gave them an imposing and depressing aspect. Almost all had been senators, procurators, or councillors; there was a multitude of uncles who had been inquisitors; those of least consequence were minor canons or *capitani grandi*. At the end of the gallery was the figure-head of the last galley fitted out against the Turks by Tiberio Aldini, Torquato's grandfather, in the days when the powerful nobles of the republic went to war at their own expense, and esteemed it glorious to place their property and persons voluntarily at the service of their country. It was a tall glass lantern, set in gilded copper, surmounted and supported by metal scroll-work of curious design, and with ornaments so placed that the bow of the vessel ended in a point. Above each portrait was a long oak bas-relief, reciting the glorious deeds of the illustrious personage beneath. It occurred to me that, if we should have war, and the opportunity should be offered me to fight for my country, I should be as patriotic and as brave as all those noble aristocrats. It seemed to me to be neither very extraordinary nor very meritorious to do great things when one was rich and powerful, and I said to myself that the trade of great nobleman could not be very difficult. But in those days, we were not at war, nor were we likely to be. The republic was merely a meaningless word, its might a mere shadow, and its enervated patricians had no elements of grandeur except their names. It was the more difficult to rise to their level in their opinion, because it was so easy to surpass them in reality. Therefore to enter into a contest with their prejudices and their contempt was unworthy of a true man, and the plebeians were fully justified in despising those among themselves who thought that they exalted themselves by seeking admission to fashionable society and aping the absurdities of the nobles.

These reflections passed through my mind confusedly at first; then they became more distinct, and I found that I could think, as I had found one fine morning that I could sing. I began to understand the repugnance I felt at the thought of leaving my proper station in life to make a spectacle of myself in society as a vain and ambitious fellow; and I determined to bury my love-affair with Bianca in the most profound mystery.

Absorbed by these reflections, I walked along the gallery, glancing proudly at that haughty race whose succession was disdained by a child of the people, a boatman from Chioggia. I felt very happy; I thought of my old father, and as I remembered the old house, long forgotten and neglected, my eyes filled with tears. I found myself at the end of the gallery, face to face with Messer Torquato, and for the first time I scrutinized him boldly from head to foot. He was the very incarnation of hereditary nobility. His glance seemed to drive one back like the point of a sword, and his hand looked as if it had never opened except to impose a command on his inferiors. I took pleasure in flouting him. "Well!" I said to him mentally, "whatever you might have done, I would never have been your servant. Your domineering air would not have frightened me, and I would have looked you in the face as I look at this canvas. You would never have obtained any hold on me, because my heart is prouder than yours ever was, because I despise this gold before which you bowed, because I am a greater man than you in the eyes of the woman you possessed. In spite of all your pride of birth, you bent the knee to her to obtain her wealth; and when you were rich through her, you crushed and humbled her. That is the conduct of a dastard, and mine is worthy of a genuine noble, for I want none of Bianca's wealth except her heart, of which you were not worthy. And I refuse what you implored, so that I may possess that which is precious above all things in my eyes, Bianca's esteem. And I shall obtain it, for she will understand the vast superiority of my heart to a debt-ridden patrician's. I have no patrimony to redeem, you see! There is no mortgage on my father's fishing-boat; and the clothes I wear are my own, because I earned them by my toil. Very good! I shall be the benefactor, not the debtor, because I shall restore happiness and life to that heart which you broke, because I, servant and lover, shall succeed in winning blessings and honor, while you, nobleman and husband, were cursed and despised."

A slight sound caused me to turn my head. I saw little Alezia behind me; she was crossing the gallery, dragging a doll larger than herself. I loved the child, despite her haughty nature, because of her love for her mother. I tried to kiss her; but, as if she felt in the atmosphere the disgrace which had been weighing upon me in that house for two days past, she drew back with an offended air, and crouched against her father's portrait, as if she had some reason to fear me. I was instantly struck by the resemblance which her pretty little dark face bore to Torquato's haughty features, and I stopped to examine her more closely, with a feeling of profound sadness. She seemed to me to be scrutinizing me attentively at the same time. Suddenly she broke the silence to say to me in a tone of great bitterness, and with an indignant expression beyond her years:

"Why have you stolen my papa's ring?"

As she spoke, she pointed with her tiny finger at a beautiful diamond ring, mounted in the old style, which her mother had given me several days before, and which I had been childish enough to accept; then she turned and, standing on tiptoe, placed her finger on one of the fingers in the portrait which was adorned with the same ring accurately copied; and I discovered that the imprudent Bianca had presented her gondolier with one of her husband's most valuable family jewels.

The blood rose in my cheeks, as I received from that child a lesson which disgusted me more than ever with ill-gotten wealth. I smiled and handed her the ring:

"Your mamma dropped it off her finger," I said, "and I found it just now in the gondola."

"I will take it to her," said the child, snatching rather than taking it from my hand. She ran away, leaving her doll on the floor. I picked up the plaything to make sure of a little circumstance which I had often noticed before. Alezia was in the habit of running a long pin through the heart of every doll she owned, and sometimes she would sit for hours at a time, absorbed in the profound and silent pleasure of that strange amusement.

In the evening Mandola came to my room. He seemed awkward and embarrassed. He had much to say to me, but he could not find a word. His expression was so curious that I roared with laughter.

"You are doing wrong, Nello," he said with a pained look on his face; "I am your friend; you are doing wrong!"

He turned to go, but I ran after him and tried to make him explain himself; it was impossible. I saw that his heart was full of sage reflections and good advice; but he lacked words in which to express himself, and all his abortive sentences, in his patois in which all languages were mingled, ended with these words:

"*E molto delica, delicatissimo.*"

At last I succeeded in making out that the rumor of my approaching marriage to the signora was current in the house. A few impatient words which some one had heard her say to Salomé were sufficient to put that rumor in circulation. The signora had said just this, speaking of me: "The time is not far away when you will take orders from him instead of giving him orders."—I obstinately denied that these words had any such meaning, and pretended that I did not understand them at all.

"Very good," said Mandola; "that's the answer you ought to make, even to me, although I am your friend. But I have eyes of my own; I don't ask you any questions, I never have done it, Nello! but I came to warn you that you must be prudent. The Aldinis are just looking for an excuse for taking the guardianship of Signora Alezia away from the signora, and she will die of grief if they take her child away from her."

"What do you say?" I cried; "what? they will take her daughter away because of me?"

"If you were to marry her, certainly," replied the

worthy gondolier; "*otherwise*—as there are some things that can't be proved,—"

"Especially when they don't exist," I rejoined warmly.

"You speak as you should speak," replied Mandola; "continue to be on your guard; trust nobody, not even me, and if you have any influence over the signora, urge her to hide her feelings, especially from Salomé. Salomé will never betray her; but her voice is too loud, and when she quarrels with the signora, everybody in the house hears what they say. If any of the signora's friends should suspect what is happening, everything would go wrong; for friends aren't like servants; they don't know how to keep a secret, and yet people trust their friends more than they do us!"

Honest Mandola's advice was not to be despised, especially as it was in perfect accord with my instinct. The next evening we took the signora to the Zueca Canal, and Mandola, understanding that I had something to say to her, obligingly fell asleep at his post. I put out the light, stole into the cabin, and talked a long while with Bianca. She was surprised by my objections and said everything that she considered likely to overcome them. I spoke firmly, I told her that I would never allow it to be said of me that I had married a woman for her wealth; that I cared as much for the good name of my family as any patrician in Venice; that my kinsmen would never forgive me if I afforded any such cause for scandal, and that I did not propose either to fall out with my dear old father or to make trouble between the signora and her daughter; for she ought to and doubtless did care more for Alezia than for all the world beside. This last argument was more powerful than any other. She burst into tears and poured forth her admiration for me and gratitude to me with the enthusiasm of passion.

From that day peace reigned once more in the Aldini Palace. That little secondary society had passed through its revolutionary crisis. It had its own peacemaker, and I laughed to myself at my rôle of great citizen, with childlike heroism. Mandola, who was beginning to acquire some education, was amazed to see me engage in the hardest sort of work, and would call me under his breath, with a paternal air, his Cincinnatus or his Pompilius.

I had in fact resolved—and I kept steadfastly to my resolution—not to accept the slightest favor from a woman whose lover I wished to be. Inasmuch as the only means of possessing her in secret was to remain in her house on the footing of a servant, it seemed to me that I could re-establish equality between her and myself by making my services correspond to my wages. Hitherto my wages had been large and entirely out of proportion to my work, which, for some time past, had been absolutely nothing. I determined to make up for lost time. I set about keeping things in order, cleaning, doing errands, bringing wood and water, polishing and brushing the gondola—in a word, doing the work of ten men ; and I did it cheerfully, humming my most beautiful operatic airs and my noblest epic strophes. The task that afforded me the most amusement was the taking care of the family pictures and brushing off the dust which obscured Torquato's majestic glance every morning. When I had completed his toilet, I would remove my cap with profound respect and ironically repeat to him some parody of my heroic verses.

The Venetian lower classes, especially the gondoliers, have, as you know, a liking for jewels. They spend a good part of what they earn in antique rings, shirt studs, scarf pins, chains and the like. I had previously accepted many trinkets of the sort. I carried them all back to Signora Aldini, and would not even wear silver buckles on my shoes. But my most meritorious sacrifice was my abandonment of music. I considered that my work, laborious as it was, was no compensation for the expense which my constant theatre-going and my singing lessons imposed on the signora. I persistently declared that I had a cold in my head, and instead of going to the performance at La Fenice with her, I adopted the practice of reading in the lobby of the theatre. I realized that I was ignorant; and, although my mistress was scarcely less so, I determined to extend my ideas a little, and not to make her blush for my blunders. I studied my mother tongue earnestly, and strove to break myself of the habit of murdering verses, as all gondoliers do. Moreover, something told me that that study would be useful to me later, and that what I lost in the way of progress in singing I should gain in the perfecting of my pronunciation and accent.

A few days of this judicious conduct served to restore my tranquillity. I had never been more manly, more cheerful, and, as Salomé said, more comely than in my neat and modest clothes, with my amiable expression and my sun-burned hands. Everybody had accorded me confidence and esteem once more, and I was again the recipient of the innumerable little attentions which I formerly enjoyed. Pretty Alezia, who had the greatest respect for the judgment of her Jewish governess, allowed me to kiss the ends of her black braids, embellished with scarlet ribbons and fine pearls.

A single person remained depressed and unhappy—the signora herself. I constantly surprised her lovely blue eyes, filled with tears, fastened upon me with an indescribable expression of affection and grief. She could not accustom herself to see me working so. If I had been her own son she could not have been more grieved to see me carrying burdens and standing in the rain. Indeed, her solicitude vexed me a little, and the efforts she made to conceal it made it even more painful to her. An entirely unforeseen revolution of sentiment had taken place in her. That love which had hitherto been, as she herself told me, her torment and her joy, seemed now to cause her naught but shame and consternation. She no longer avoided opportunities to be alone with me, as she used to do; on the contrary, she sought them; but, as soon as I knelt at her feet, she would burst into sobs and change the hours promised to the joys of love into hours of painful emotion. I strove in vain to understand what was taking place in her heart. I could obtain nothing but vague replies, always kind and affectionate, but incoherent, which caused me the utmost perplexity. I had no idea what to do to comfort her and strengthen that discouraged heart. I was consumed by desire, and it seemed to me that an hour of mutual effusion and passion would have been more eloquent than all that talk and all those tears; but I felt too much respect and devotion for her not to sacrifice my transports of passion to her. I felt that it would be very easy to take her by surprise, weak as she was in body and mind; but I dreaded the tears of the next day too much, and I wished to owe my happiness to her confidence and love alone. That day did not come, and I must say, to the discredit of feminine weakness, that, if I had shown less delicacy and unselfishness, my desires would have been fully gratified. I had hoped that Bianca would encourage me; I soon discovered that, on the contrary, she was afraid of me, and that she shuddered at my approach, as if crime and remorse approached with me. I succeeded in reassuring her only to see her plunge into still deeper dejection, and upbraid fate, as if it had not been in her power to put a better face upon her destiny. Then, too, a secret sense of shame helped to crush that shrinking heart. Religion took possession of her more and more completely; her confessor controlled her and terrified her. He forbade her to have lovers, and, although she resisted him when it was a question of Signor Lanfranchi and Signor Montalegri, she had not the same courage with respect to me. I succeeded little by little in extorting from her a confession of all her sufferings and internal struggles. She had confessed to the confessor all the details of our love, and he had declared that that low, criminal affection was a heinous crime. He had forbidden her to think of marriage with me, even more peremptorily than to give way to her passion; and he had frightened her so by threatening to cast her out from the bosom of the Church, that her gentle, timid mind, torn between the desire to make me happy and the fear of destroying her own soul, was suffering veritable agony.

Hitherto Signora Aldini's piety had been so pliant, so tolerant, so truly Italian, that I was not a little surprised to see it become serious just at the height of one of those paroxysms of passion which seem most inconsistent with such changes. I worked hard with my poor inexperienced brain to understand this phenomenon, and I succeeded. Bianca probably loved me more than she had loved the count and the prince; but she had not sufficient courage nor a sufficiently enlightened mind to rise above public opinion. She complained of the arrogance of other people; but she gave real value to that arrogance by her fear of it. In a word, she was more submissive than anybody else to the prejudice which she had attempted for an instant to defy. She had hoped to find in the church, through the sacrament, and by redoubling her pious fervor, the strength which she failed to find in herself, and which she had not needed with her former lovers, because they were patricians and society was on their side. But now the church threatened her, society would heap maledictions upon her; to fight against the church and society at the same time was a task beyond her strength.

Then too, it may be that her love subsided as soon as I became worthy of it; perhaps, instead of appreciating the grandeur of soul which had led me to descend of my own motion from the salon to the servant's quarters, she had fancied that she could detect in that courageous behavior a lack of dignity and an inborn liking for servitude. She believed too that the threats and sarcasms of her other servants had frightened me. She was astonished to find that I was not ambitious, and that very absence of ambition seemed to her an indication of an inert or timid spirit. She did not admit all this to me; but as soon as I was once on the track I divined it all. I was not angry. How could she understand my noble pride and my sensitive honor, she who had accepted and returned the love of an Aldini and a Lanfranchi?

Doubtless she ceased to consider me handsome when I refused to wear lace and ribbons. My hands, calloused in her service, no longer seemed to her worthy to press hers. She had loved me as a gondolier, in the thought and hope of transforming me into an attractive cicisbeo; but the instant that I insisted upon reverting to the system of a fair exchange of services between her and myself, all her illusions vanished, and she saw in me only the vulgar fisherman's son of Chioggia, a species of stupid and hard-working beast of burden.

As these discoveries cleared the mists away from my mind, the violence of my passions diminished. If I had had to deal with a great soul, or even with a forceful nature, it would have been in my eyes a glorious task to efface the distressing memories left behind in that heart by my predecessors. But to succeed such men simply to be misunderstood, and in all probability to be some day cast aside and forgotten like them, was a happiness which I no longer cared to purchase at the cost of an enormous expenditure of passion and will-power. Signora Aldini was a sweet and lovely woman; but could I not find in a cottage at Chioggia beauty and sweetness united, without causing tears to flow, without causing remorse, and above all without leaving shame behind me?

My mind was soon made up. I resolved not only to leave the signora, but to cease to be a servant. So long as I had been in love with her harp and her person, I had had no time to reflect seriously on my condition. But, as soon as I abandoned my foolish aspirations, I realized how difficult it is to retain one's dignity unimpaired under the protection of the great, and I recalled the salutary arguments which my father had urged upon me, and to which I had paid little heed.

When I gave her an inkling of my purpose, I saw, although she opposed it, that she was greatly relieved; happiness might return and dwell once more in that affectionate and beneficent heart. The charming frivolity which was the basis of her character would reappear on the surface with the first lover who should be able to push aside her confessor, her servants, and society. A great passion would have shattered her system; a succession of mild passions and a multitude of lukewarm attachments would keep her alive in her natural element.

I forced her to admit all that I had divined. She had never studied herself very much, and she was always most sincere. If there was no heroism in her character, neither was there any pretension to heroism, nor the overbearing despotism which is its consequence. She approved my determination, but she wept and was dismayed at the thought of the blank my departure would leave in her life; for she loved me still, I am sure, with all the strength of her nature.

She attempted to worry and fret about what was to become of me. I would not allow it. The abrupt and haughty tone in which I interrupted her when she spoke of offering her services closed her mouth once for all in that respect. I would not even take the clothes she had had made for me. On the day before I was to take my leave, I purchased the complete outfit of a sailor of Chioggia, new, but of the coarsest materials; and in that guise I appeared before her for the last time.

She had requested me to come to her at midnight, so that we could part without witnesses. I was grateful to her for the affectionate familiarity with which she embraced me. I do not believe there was another society woman in all Venice sufficiently sincere and sympathetic to be willing to repeat the assurance of her love to a man dressed as I was. Tears poured from her eyes when she passed her little white hands over the rough material of my scarlet-lined cape; then she smiled, and, pulling the hood over my head, gazed at me lovingly, and exclaimed that she had never seen me look so handsome, and that she had done very wrong ever to make me dress in any other way. The warmth and sincerity of my thanks, the oaths I took to be faithful to her until death, and never to think of her except to bless her and commend her to God's keeping, touched her deeply. She was not accustomed to being left in that way.

"You have a more chivalrous heart," she said to me, "than any of those who bear the title of chevalier."

Then she gave way to an outburst of enthusiasm: the

independence of my nature, the indifference with which I laid aside luxury and indolence for the hardest of lives, the respect with which I had never failed to treat her when it would have been so easy for me to abuse her weakness for me; all this, she said, raised me far above other men. She threw herself into my arms, almost at my feet, and again begged me not to go away, but to marry her.

This outburst was sincere, and, although it did not change my resolution, it made the signora so lovely and so fascinating that I was very near casting my heroism to the winds and taking my reward in that last night for all the sacrifices I had made to my peace of mind. But I had the strength to resist, and to go forth chaste from a love affair which nevertheless had its origin in sensual desire. I took my leave, bathed in her tears, and carrying away, as my sole treasure and trophy, a lock of her lovely fair hair. As I withdrew I went to little Alezia's bed, and softly put aside the curtains to take a last look at her. She at once woke, and did not recognize me at first, for she was frightened; she did not cry out, but simply called her mother in a voice which she tried to keep from trembling.

"Signorina," I said, "I am the *Orco*,* and I have come to ask you why you pierce the hearts of your dolls with pins."

She sat up in bed, and replied, glancing at me with a mischievous expression:

"I do it to see if their blood is blue."

Blue blood, you know, is synonymous with noble in the popular language of Venice.

"But they have no blood," I said; "they are not noble!"

* The red devil, or will'o-the-wisp of the lagoons.

"They are nobler than you," was her retort, "for their blood isn't black."

Black, you know, is the color of the *nicoloti,* the association of boatmen.

"*Signora mia,*" I said in an undertone to her mother, as I drew the child's curtains, "you have done well not to splash ink on your azure crest. Here is a little patrician who would never have forgiven you."

"And my heart," she replied sadly, "is pierced, not with a pin, but with a thousand swords."

When I was in the street, I stopped to look at the corner of the palace which stood out in the moonlight from the eaves to the depths of the Grand Canal. A boat passed, and, causing a ripple in the water, cut and scattered the reflection of that pure line. It seemed to me that I had just had a beautiful dream and had awakened in darkness. I began to run at full speed, never looking behind, and did not stop until I reached the Paglia bridge, where the boats for Chioggia await passengers, while the boatmen, wrapped in their capes in winter and summer alike, lie sound asleep on the parapet, and even across the steps, under the feet of passers-by. I asked if anyone of my fellow-townsmen would take me to my father's house.

"Is it you, *kinsman?*" they cried in surprise.

That word *kinsman,* which the Venetians ironically bestow on the Chioggians, and which the latter have had the good-sense to accept,* was so sweet to my ear that I embraced the first man who called me by it. They promised to start in an hour, and asked me several questions, but did not listen to my answers. The Chioggian hardly knows the use of a bed; but he sleeps while walking,

* The peninsula of Chioggia was originally inhabited by five or six families which never married except among themselves.

talking, even rowing. They suggested my taking a nap on the common bed, that is to say on the flagstones of the quay. I lay on the ground, with my head on one of those worthy fellows, while another used me as a pillow, and so on. I slept as in the happiest days of my childhood, and I dreamed that my poor mother—who had been dead a year—appeared in the doorway of our cottage and congratulated me on my return. I was awakened by the repeated shouts of *Chiosa! Chiosa!** with which our boatmen wake the echoes of the ducal palace and the prisons, to attract passengers. It seemed to me a cry of triumph, like the *Italia! Italia!* of the Trojans in the *Æneid*. I jumped aboard a boat with a light heart, and, thinking of the night Bianca must have passed, reproached myself a little for sleeping soundly. But I was reconciled to myself by the thought that I had not poisoned her future peace of mind.

It was midwinter and the nights were long; we reached Chioggia an hour before dawn. I ran to our cabin. My father was already at sea; only my youngest brother was left behind to look after the house. It took a long while for him to wake up and recognize me. It was easy to see that he was accustomed to sleep amid the roar of the waves and the storm; for I nearly broke the door down trying to make him hear me. At last he came out, leaped on my neck, put on his cape and rowed me half a league out to sea, to the spot where my father's boat lay at anchor. The excellent man, awaiting the best time to set his nets, was asleep, according to the custom of old fishermen, stretched out on his back, his body and face sheltered by a coarse blanket, while the stinging north wind whistled through the rigging. The white-capped waves beat against the vessel and covered him with spray;

* Chioggia!

no human voice could be heard in the vast solitude of the
Adriatic. I softly put aside the blanket and looked at
him. He was the image of strength in repose. His gray
beard, as tangled as the seaweed when the tide is rising,
his earth-colored jacket and his dull green woollen cap
made him resemble an old Triton asleep in his shell.
He displayed no more surprise when he woke than if he
had been expecting me.

"Oho!" he said, "I was dreaming of the poor woman,
and she said to me: 'Get up, old man, here's our son
Daniel back again.'"

SECOND PART

I do not propose, my friends, to describe all the vicissi-
tudes which marked my passage from the beach at Chioggia to the stage of the leading theatres in Italy, and
from the trade of fisherman to the rôle of *primo tenore;*
that was the work of several years, and my reputation
increased rapidly as soon as I had taken the first step in
my career. If circumstances were often unfavorable,
my easy-going disposition was always able to make the
best of them, and I can fairly say that my great suc-
cesses did not cost me very dear.

Ten years after leaving Venice, I was at Naples, playing Romeo at the San Carlo theatre. King Murat and
his brilliant staff, and all the vain and venal beauties of
Italy, were there. I did not pride myself on being a
particularly ardent patriot, but I did not share the infatu-
ation of that period for foreign domination. I did not

turn my face backward toward a still more degrading past; I fed upon the first elements of Carbonarism, which were then fermenting, without definite shape or name, from Prussia to Sicily.

My heroism was simple and intense, as all religions are at their birth. I carried into all that I did, and especially into my art, the feeling of mocking pride and democratic independence which inspired me every day in the clubs and in clandestine pamphlets. *Friends of Truth, Friends of Light, Friends of Liberty*—such were the names under which liberal sympathies gathered; and even in the ranks of the French army, at the very side of the victorious leaders, we had associates, children of your great revolution, who, in their secret hearts, were determined to wash away the stain of the 18th Brumaire.

I loved the rôle of Romeo, because I could give expression in it to warlike sentiments and feelings of chivalrous detestation. When my audience, always half French, applauded my dramatic outbursts, I felt as if I were revenged for our national degradation; for those conquerors were unconsciously applauding curses aimed at them, longings for their death and threats to attain it.

One evening, during one of my finest moments, when it seemed as if the roof would fall under the explosions of frantic applause, my eyes fell upon a face in a proscenium box almost on the stage, an impassive face, the sight of which made my blood suddenly run cold. You have no idea of the mysterious influences which govern the actor's inspiration, how the expression of certain faces absorbs him, and stimulates or deadens his audacity. Speaking for myself at least, I cannot avoid an instant sympathy with my audience, whether the effect is to spur me on if I find it inclined to resist, until

I subjugate it by my passion, or to melt us into one as by the action of an electric current, so that its quick response imparts new vigor to my sensitive talent. But certain glances, or certain words spoken in whispers close beside me, have sometimes disturbed me so that it required the utmost effort of which my will was capable to combat their effect.

The face that impressed me at that moment was ideally beautiful; its owner was beyond dispute the most beautiful woman in the whole theatre. Meanwhile, the whole audience was roaring and stamping in admiration, and she alone, the queen of the evening, seemed to be studying me dispassionately, and to discover faults which the vulgar eye could not detect. She was the Muse of Tragedy, stern Melpomene in person, with her regular oval face, her black eyebrows, her high forehead, her raven hair, her great eyes gleaming with a dark flame in their vast orbits, and her stern lip, whose unbending curve was never softened by a smile; and, with all the rest, in the very bloom and flower of youth, with a graceful, lithe figure instinct with health.

"Who is that lovely dark girl with such a cold eye?" I asked Count Nasi, during the entr'acte; he had taken a great liking to me, and came on the stage every evening to chat with me.

"She is either the daughter or niece of Princess Grimani," was his reply. "I do not know her, for she has just come from some convent or other, and her mother, or aunt, is herself a stranger in this region. All I can tell you is that Prince Grimani loves her like his own child, that he will give her a handsome dowry, and that she is one of the richest matches in Italy; and yet I shall never take my place in the lists."

"Why not, pray?"

"Because they say she is insolent and vain, infatuated with her noble birth, and of an overbearing disposition. I care so little for women of that stamp that I don't even care to look at her when I meet her. They say that she will be queen of the balls next winter, and that her beauty is something marvellous. I don't know or want to know whether it is or is not. I can't endure Grimani either; he is a genuine stage *hidalgo;* and if it were not that he has a handsome fortune and a young wife who is said to be attractive, I don't know how anyone could be induced to endure the tedium of his conversation or the freezing stiffness of his hospitality."

During the following scene I glanced at the proscenium box from time to time. I was no longer disturbed by the thought that its occupants were disposed to judge me unfavorably, since I had learned that the Grimanis were accustomed to maintain a haughty demeanor even with people whom they considered to belong to their own class. I looked at the girl with the impartiality of a sculptor or a painter; she seemed to me even lovelier than at first sight. Old Grimani, who was sitting beside her at the front of the box, had a fine face, but stern and cold. That supercilious couple seemed to exchange a few monosyllables at long intervals, and at the end of the opera he rose slowly and went out, without waiting for the ballet.

The next day the old man and the young woman were in the same place, in the same unmoved attitude. I did not once see any trace of emotion, and Prince Grimani slept sweetly throughout the first acts. The young woman, on the contrary, seemed to be paying her whole attention to the performance. Her great eyes were fastened on me like those of a ghost, and that fixed, searching and profound gaze became so embarrassing to me that I carefully avoided it. But, as if an evil spell had been cast upon me, the more I tried to keep my eyes away, the more they persisted in meeting those of the young sorceress. There was something so extraordinarily powerful in that mysterious magnetism, that I was assailed by childish dread of it, and feared that I should not be able to finish the opera. I had never felt anything like it. There were times when I fancied that I recognized that marble face, and I seemed to be on the point of accosting her as an old friend. At other times I believed that she was my deadly enemy, my evil genius, and I was tempted to hurl violent reproaches at her.

The *seconda donna* added to my truly alarming discomfort by whispering to me:

"Look out, Lelio, you'll catch the fever. That woman in the box will give you the *jettatura*."*

I had been a firm believer in the *jettatura* during the greater part of my life. I no longer believed in it; but the love of the marvellous, which is not easily dislodged from an Italian head, especially that of a child of the people, had led me to indulge in most extravagant reflections on the subject of animal magnetism. It was the period when charming fancies of that sort were blooming luxuriantly all over the world; Hoffmann was writing his *Tales*, and magnetism was the mysterious pivot upon which all the hopes of the *illuminati* turned. Whether because that foible had taken such complete possession of me that it controlled my actions, or because it took me by surprise at a moment when I was not in the best of health, I began to shiver from head to foot, and I nearly fainted when I returned to the stage. That wretched

* The glance of the evil eye. This superstition is common all over Italy. At Naples they wear coral talismans as a safeguard.

weakness finally gave place to wrath, and as I walked toward the box in question with La Checchina—the *seconda donna* who had mentioned the evil eye—I said to her, indicating my fair enemy, but in a tone too low to be overheard by the audience, these words paraphrased from one of our finest tragedies :

"*Bella e stupida.*"

The signora flushed to the roots of her hair with anger. She started to rouse Prince Grimani, who was sleeping with all his heart ; but she suddenly stopped, as if she had changed her mind, and kept her eyes fixed upon me as before, but with a vindictive, threatening expression which seemed to say :

"You shall repent of that."

Count Nasi accosted me as I left the theatre after the performance.

"Lelio," said he, "you are in love with the Grimani."

"Am I bewitched, in God's name," I cried, "and why is it that I cannot rid myself of that apparition ? "

"You won't rid yourself of it for a long time either, poor boy," said Checchina, with a half-artless, half-mocking air ; "that Grimani is the devil. Wait a moment," she added, taking my arm, "I know something about fever, and I will wager—*Corpo della Madonna!*"— she cried, turning pale, "you have a terrible attack of fever, my poor Lelio ! "

"One always has the fever when one acts and sings in a way to give it to others," said the count ; "come to supper with me, Lelio."

I declined ; I was ill, in very truth. During the night I had a violent fever, and the next day I could not leave my bed. Checchina installed herself at my bedside and did not leave me all the time that I was ill.

Checchina was a young woman of twenty or thereabout, tall and large, and of a somewhat masculine type of beauty, although very white and fair. She was my sister and my kinswoman, that is to say, she came from Chioggia. Like me she was a fisherman's child and had long employed her strength beating the waters of the Adriatic with oars. A wild love of independence led her to use her fine voice as a means of assuring herself a free profession and a wandering life. She had run away from her father's house and begun to roam about the country on foot, singing in the public squares. I chanced to meet her at Milan, in a furnished lodging-house where she was singing for the guests at the table d'hôte. I recognized her as a Chioggian by her accent; I questioned her and remembered seeing her as a child; but I was careful to say nothing by which she could identify me as a *kinsman*, especially as that Daniele Gemello who had left the neighborhood rather suddenly, as the result of an unlucky duel. That duel cost a poor devil his life and his murderer many sleepless nights.

Allow me to pass rapidly over that incident, and to avoid awakening a bitter memory during our quiet evening. It will be enough for me to say to Zorzi that the practice of duelling with knives was still in full vigor at Chioggia in my youth, and the whole population acted as seconds. Duels were fought in broad daylight, on the public square, and insults were avenged by the wager of combat, as in the days of chivalry. My melancholy success exiled me from the province! for the *podestat* was far from lenient in such matters, and the law inflicted severe penalties upon the last remnants of those savage old customs. Perhaps this will explain why I always concealed the story of my early years, and why I travelled over the world under the name of Lelio, sending money secretly to my family, writing to them with the greatest caution, and disclosing to no one, not even to them, my means of subsistence, for fear that, by corresponding with me they might draw upon themselves the open hostility of those families in Chioggia whom the death of my assailant had angered more or less.

But, as my origin was betrayed by an ineradicable trace of the Venetian accent, I passed myself off as a native of Palestrina, and Checchina had adopted the habit of calling me her *countryman,* her *cousin* or her *gossip,* as it happened.

Thanks to my care and my assistance, Checchina rapidly acquired considerable talent, and at the time of my life of which I am now speaking, she had been engaged on honorable terms as a member of the troupe at San Carlo.

She was a strange but most excellent creature, was Checchina; she had improved wonderfully since I had picked her out of the gutter, so to speak; but she still retained, and retains to this day, a certain rusticity which does not altogether disappear on the stage, and which makes her the first actress in the world in such rôles as Zerlina. She had corrected in large measure the amplitude of her gestures and the abruptness of her speech, but she retained enough of both to come very near being comic in pathetic parts. However, as she had intelligence and feeling, she raised herself to a relatively high position, but the public did not give her all the credit she deserved. Opinions were divided concerning her, and a certain abbé said that she brushed so close to the sublime and the farcical that there was not enough room left between the two for her long arms.

Unluckily, Checchina had one failing, from which, by the way, the greatest artists are not exempt. She satisfied herself only in rôles which were entirely unsuited to her, and, scorning those in which she could best display her *verve,* her unconstant and her restless activity, she insisted upon producing great effects in tragedy. Like a true village maiden, she was intoxicated by superb costumes, and fancied that she was really a queen when she wore a diadem and a royal cloak. Her tall, lithe figure, her graceful, quasi-martial bearing, made of her a magnificent statue when she was not in motion. But her exaggerated gestures constantly betrayed the young oarswoman, and when I desired, on the stage, to warn her to be less vehement, I would whisper: *"Per dio! non vogar! non siamo qui sull' Adriatico."**

Whether Checchina was my mistress is a question of little interest to you, I presume. I can only assure you that she was not at the time of which I am speaking, and that I was indebted for her affectionate care to nothing else than the kindness of her heart and her unfailing gratitude. She has always been a devoted sister and friend to me, and many a time she has risked a rupture with her most brilliant lovers, rather than desert me or neglect me when my health or my interests demanded her zealous care or her aid.

As I was saying, she took up her post at my bedside, and did not leave me until she had cured me. Her tireless devotion to me vexed Count Nasi somewhat, although he was my friend and placed full confidence in my word; but he himself confessed to me what he called his miserable weakness. When I urged Checchina to deal more gently with that excellent young man's involuntary sensitiveness, she would say:

"Nonsense! Don't you see that I must train him to respect my independence? Do you suppose that, when I am his wife, I will consent to abandon my stage friends

* In God's name, don't row! we are not on the Adriatic.

and worry about what people in society think of me? Don't believe it, Lelio. I propose to remain free, and to obey the voice of my heart and nothing else."

She had persuaded herself, with none too good reason, that the count was fully determined to marry her; and I may say that she possessed, to a marvellous degree, the gift of deluding herself with respect to the violence of the passions she inspired; nothing could equal her confidence in a promise, unless it were her philosophical and heroic indifference when she was deceived.

I suffered considerably; my disease came very near assuming a serious character. The doctors found a very pronounced tendency to enlargement of the heart, and the very sharp pains which I felt about that organ and the excessive rush of blood thither necessitated numerous bleedings. So that I lost the rest of that season, and, as soon as I was convalescent, I went for rest and balmy air to a beautiful villa of Count Nasi's, a few leagues from Florence, near Cafaggiolo, at the foot of the Apennines. He promised to join me there with Checchina as soon as the performances for which she was engaged would allow her to leave Naples.

A few days of that delightful solitude benefited me so much that I was allowed to take excursions of some length, sometimes in the saddle, sometimes on foot, through the narrow gorges and picturesque ravines which form a first step to the towering masses of the Apennines. In my musing I called that region the *proscenium* of the great range, and I loved to seek out some amphitheatre of hills or some natural terrace where, all alone and far from every eye, I could indulge in outbursts of lyric declamation, which were answered by the resonant echoes or the mysterious murmur of the streams flowing under the rocks.

One day I unexpectedly found myself on the Florence road. Like a glistening white ribbon it ran through a verdant, gently undulating country, strewn with beautiful gardens, wooded parks and handsome villas. Seeking to learn my whereabouts, I stopped at the gate of one of those charming abodes. The gate was open, and I could see an avenue of old trees mysteriously intertwined. Beneath those dark, voluptuously enlaced branches a woman was walking slowly—a woman of slender form and a bearing so noble that I paused to gaze at her and follow her with my eyes as long as possible. As she showed no inclination to turn, I was seized with an irresistible longing to see her features, and I yielded to it, heedless of the fact that I was violating the proprieties, and might be subjected to a humiliating rebuff.

"Who can say," I said to myself, "women are so indulgent sometimes in this mild climate of ours!"

Moreover, I reasoned that my face was too well known for me ever to be taken for a robber; and, lastly, I relied to some extent on the curiosity which the great majority of people feel to obtain a near view of the features and manners of an artist of some celebrity.

So I ventured into the shady avenue, walking rapidly, and was just about to overtake the solitary promenader, when I saw coming toward her a young man dressed in the latest fashion, and with a pretty, insipid face, who caught sight of me before I had time to jump in among the trees. I was within three yards of the noble pair. The young man stopped beside the lady, offered her his arm, and said to her, glancing at me with the most surprised air of which a perfectly attired man is capable:

"My dear cousin, who is this man who is following you?"

The lady turned, and the sight of her gave me such a

shock that for a moment I was in danger of a relapse. My heart gave a sharp, nervous throb as I recognized the young woman who stared at me in such a curious way from her proscenium box at the time I was taken ill at Naples. Her face flushed slightly, then lost its color. But no gesture, no exclamation betrayed either surprise or anger. She eyed me from head to foot with calm disdain, and replied with incredible audacity:

"I don't know him."

That extraordinary statement aroused my curiosity. It seemed to me that I could detect in that girl such consummate dissimulation and such a strange sort of pride that I suddenly felt irresistibly impelled to take the risk of a mad adventure. We Bohemians do not allow ourselves to be awed overmuch by the customs of society and the laws of propriety; we have no great fear of being ejected from those private theatres where society takes its turn at posing before us, and where we feel so strongly the superiority of the artist; for there no one can arouse in us the intense emotions which we have the art of arousing. Salons bore us to death and chill our blood, in return for the warmth and life that we carry thither. So I approached my noble hosts with a dignified air, caring very little about the manner of their reception of me, and determined to take the first convenient pretext for obtaining admission to the house.

I bowed gravely and represented myself as a piano-tuner who had been sent for to Florence from a country-house, the name of which I pretended to remember imperfectly.

"This is not the place. You may quit this place," replied the signora, coldly. But, like a true fiancé, the cousin came to my assistance.

"My dear cousin," he said, "your piano is terribly out

of tune; if this man could spare an hour, we might have some music this evening. I beg you to let him tune it, won't you?"

The young Grimani had a wicked smile on her lips as she replied:

"As you please, cousin."

"Does she propose to amuse herself at my expense or his?" I thought. "Perhaps both."

I bowed slightly to signify my consent. Thereupon the cousin, with careless courtesy, pointed out to me a glass door at the end of the avenue, where the branches, drooping lower and lower until they formed a sort of arbor, concealed the front of the villa.

"At the end of the large salon, signor," he said, "you will find a study. The piano is there. I shall have the honor to see you again when you have finished. Shall we walk as far as the pond?" he added, turning to his cousin.

I saw her smile again, almost imperceptibly, but with the keenest delight at the mortification that I felt, while she let me go in one direction and continued her stroll in the other, leaning on the arm of her elegant and aristocratic cousin.

It is not a very difficult matter to put a piano *almost* in tune, and although I had never tried before, I succeeded very well; but I spent much more time about it than an experienced hand would have required, and I watched with some impatience the sun sinking behind the tree-tops; for I had no other pretext for another interview with my singular heroine than to hear her try the piano when it was in tune. So I worked away awkwardly enough, and was in the midst of a monotonous drumming with which I was almost deafening myself, when I raised my head and saw the signora before me, half turned toward the fireplace, but watching me in the mirror with malicious intentness. To meet her sidelong glance and turn my eyes away was a matter of a second. I continued my work with the utmost coolness, resolved to watch the enemy and see what she was driving at.

La Grimani—I continued to give her that name in my mind, knowing no other—made a pretence of arranging some flowers in the vases on the mantel with great care; then she moved a chair, moved it back to the place where it was before, dropped her fan, picked it up with a great rustling of her skirts, opened a window, and instantly closed it again, then, seeing that I was determined not to notice anything, she adopted the extreme course of dropping a stool on her pretty little foot and uttering a cry of pain. I was stupid enough to drop the key on the metallic strings, which emitted a piteous wail. The signora started, shrugged her shoulders, and, suddenly recovering all her self-possession, as if we were acting a scene in a burlesque, she looked me in the face and said:

"*Cosa, signore?*"

"I thought that your ladyship spoke to me," I replied, with no less tranquillity, and resumed my work. She remained standing in the middle of the room as if petrified by amazement in the face of such audacity, or as if brought to a standstill by a sudden doubt as to my identity with the person whom she had thought that she recognized. At last she lost patience, and asked me, almost roughly, if I had nearly finished.

"Oh! bless my soul, no! signora," I replied; "here is a broken string, you see." As I spoke I gave the key a sharp twist on the pin I was turning, and broke the string.

"It seems to me," said she, "that this piano is giving you a great deal of trouble."

"A great deal," I rejoined, "the strings keep breaking." And I snapped a second one.

"That is very extraordinary," she exclaimed.

"Yes, it is indeed extraordinary," I replied.

The cousin entered at that moment, and I snapped a third string by way of salute. It was one of the lower bass strings, and it made a terrible report. The cousin, who was not expecting it, stepped back, and the signora laughed aloud. That laugh had a strange sound to me. It was not in harmony with her face or her manner; it was harsh and spasmodic, and disconcerted the cousin so that I almost pitied him.

"I am very much afraid," she said, when that nervous paroxysm came to an end and she was able to speak, "I am very much afraid that we cannot have any music to-night. This poor old *cembalo* is bewitched, all the strings are breaking. It is really supernatural, I assure you, Hector; if you so much as look at them they twist and snap with a horrible noise."

With that she began to laugh again, peal upon peal, without the slightest trace of merriment on her face. The cousin laughed because she did, but was abruptly checked by these words from her;

"For heaven's sake, cousin, don't laugh; you haven't the slightest inclination to."

The cousin seemed to me to be well used to being laughed at and teased. But he was hurt, no doubt, to be treated so in my presence; for he said in an irritated tone:

"Why shouldn't I be inclined to laugh as well as you, cousin?"

"Because I say that you are not," she replied. "But tell me, Hector," she added, abruptly changing the subject, "were you at San Carlo last year?"

"No, cousin."

" In that case you did not hear the famous Lelio ? "
She said these last words with significant emphasis ; but she had not the impudence to look me in the face immediately, and I had time to recover from the emotion caused me by that blow full in the face.

"I neither heard him nor saw him," said the guileless cousin, " but I heard a great deal about him. He's a great artist, so I understand."

" Very great," replied La Grimani, " a full head taller than you. See! he is about this gentleman's height.—Do you know him, signor ? " she added, turning to me.

"I know him very well, signora," I replied tartly ; " he is a very handsome fellow, a very great actor, an admirable singer, a very clever talker, a bold and spirited adventurer, and, furthermore, a fearless duellist, which is not amiss."

The signora looked at her cousin, then glanced at me, with an indifferent air, as if to say : " It's of little consequence to me." Then she went off into another paroxysm of inextinguishable laughter, which was altogether unnatural, and in which neither her cousin nor myself joined. I returned to my pursuit of the dominant chord on the keyboard, and Signor Ettore moved about impatiently, making his new boots squeak on the floor, as if he were utterly disgusted with the conversation being carried on between a mere workman like myself and his noble fiancée.

"Look you, cousin, you mustn't believe what he says about Lelio," observed the signora, abruptly ceasing her convulsive laughter. " So far as the man's great beauty is concerned, I cannot contradict him for I didn't look at him ; and, besides, an actor can always appear young and handsome with his paint and his false hair and moustaches. But as to his being an admirable singer and a good actor, that I deny. In the first place he sings false, in the second place he acts detestably. His declamation is too loud, his gestures commonplace, the expression of his features stiff and conventional. When he weeps, he makes wry faces; when he threatens, he roars; when he is majestic, he is tedious; and, in his best moments, when he holds himself back and doesn't speak, one might apply to him the refrain of the ballad:

" *'Brutto è quanto stupido.'*

I am sorry to disagree with this gentleman; but my opinion is the opinion of the public! It isn't my fault that Lelio didn't have the slightest success at San Carlo, and I don't advise you to take the journey to Naples to see him, cousin."

Having received this stinging lesson, for a moment I was on the verge of losing my head and picking a quarrel with the cousin to punish the signora; but the excellent youth did not give me time.

"That is just like a woman," he cried, "and above all things just like one of your inconceivable whims, cousin! Not more than three days ago, you told me that Lelio was the finest actor and the most incomparable singer in all Italy. I have no doubt that you will say to-morrow just the opposite of what you say to-day, with the privilege of taking it all back again the next day."

"To-morrow and the day after to-morrow and every day of my life, my dear cousin," the signora hurriedly interposed, "I will tell you that you are a fool and Lelio an idiot."

"Brava, signora," rejoined the cousin in an undertone, offering her his arm to leave the salon; "he who loves you is a fool, and he who displeases you an idiot."

"Before your lordship and ladyship retire," I said,

without the slightest symptom of emotion, "I will call your attention to the fact that this piano is in such a bad condition that I cannot possibly repair it properly in one day. I am obliged to go now; but if such is your wish, I will return to-morrow."

"Certainly, signor," replied the cousin, with patronizing politeness, half turning toward me; "you will oblige me if you will return to-morrow."

La Grimani, stopping him with a sudden and energetic motion of her head, forced him to turn wholly around, and as she stood in the doorway, leaning on his arm and eyeing me with an air of defiance, she said, as she saw me close the piano and take my hat:

"Will the signor come again to-morrow?"

"Most certainly I shall not fail to do so," I replied, bowing to the ground.

She continued to detain her cousin in the doorway, so that I was obliged to pass in front of them in order to go out; and, as I did so, I bowed again and looked my Bradamante in the eye with an assurance befitting the combat upon which we had entered. A gleam of undaunted courage flashed from her eyes. Therein I read distinctly that my boldness did not displease her, and that the lists were not closed to me.

So I was at my post before noon the next day, and found my heroine at hers, seated at the piano and touching the silent or jangling keys with admirable indifference, as if she desired to prove to me by those diabolical discords her detestation and contempt for music.

I entered calmly and saluted her with as much respectful indifference as if I were in reality a piano-tuner. I placed my hat carelessly on a chair, I laboriously drew off my gloves, imitating the awkwardness of a man unused to wearing them. I took from my pocket a wooden box filled with spools of wire, and began to unwind enough for one string—all with the utmost gravity and without affectation. The signora continued to pound the hapless piano in unmerciful fashion, although the sounds she produced were of a nature to put to flight the most hardened savages. I at once saw that she was amusing herself by destroying its tone and breaking it more and more, in order to provide work for me, and I detected more coquetry than cruelty in that devilment; for she seemed disposed to remain with me.

Thereupon I said to her with a perfectly serious face: "Does your ladyship think that the piano begins to be in tune?"

"The harmony is satisfactory to me," she said, biting her lips to keep from laughing, "and the sounds it gives forth are extremely pleasant to the ear."

"It is a fine instrument," said I.

"And in very good condition," she rejoined.

"Your ladyship is a very talented performer."

"As you see."

"That is a charming waltz, and exceedingly well executed."

"Is it not? How could one help playing well on an instrument in such perfect tune? You love music, signor?"

"A little, signora; but your playing goes to my heart."

"In that case I will continue." And she proceeded, with a fiendish smile, to murder one of the *bravura* airs she had heard me sing with the greatest applause on the stage.

"Is his lordship your cousin well?" I said, when she had finished.

"He is hunting."

"Is your ladyship fond of game?"
"I am immoderately fond of it. And you, signor?"
"I am sincerely and deeply partial to it."
"Which do you like best, game or music?"
"I like music at table, but at this moment I should like some game better."

She rose and rang. A servant appeared instantly, as if he were a piece of machinery set in motion by the bell-rope.

"Bring the game-pie that I saw in the pantry this morning," said the signora; and two minutes later the servant reappeared with an enormous pie, which he majestically placed on the piano at a sign from his mistress. A large salver, covered with dishes and all the accessories necessary for the refreshment of civilized beings, appeared as if by magic on the other side of the instrument, and the signora, with a strong but light touch, broke through the rampart of appetizing crust and made a large breach in the fortress.

"This is a conquest in which our lords and masters the French shall have no share," she said, taking possession of a partridge which she placed on a Japanese plate; and she went with it to the other end of the room, where she squatted upon a velvet hassock with gold tassels, and proceeded to devour it.

I gazed at her in amazement, uncertain whether she was mad or was trying to mystify me.

"You are not eating?" she said, without moving.

"Your ladyship has not ordered me to do so," I replied.

"Oh! don't stand on ceremony," said she, continuing to eat with great zest.

The pie had such an alluring look and such a delicious odor that I listened to the philosophical arguments of common sense. I placed another partridge on another

Japanese plate, which I rested on the keyboard of the piano, and began to eat with as much gusto as the signora.

"If this is not the castle of the Sleeping Beauty," I thought, "and if this cruel fairy is not the only living being in it, we shall soon see an uncle or a father or an aunt or a governess, or somebody who is supposed, in the eyes of honest folk, to serve as chaperon to this untamed creature. In case of any such apparition, I should like to know just how far this eccentric fashion of breakfasting on a piano, tête-à-tête with the young lady of the house, will be considered seemly. It matters little after all; I must find out just where these extravagant whims are likely to carry me, and if there is a woman's spite behind them, I will have my turn if I have to wait ten years."

As I reflected thus I watched my fair hostess over the piano. She was eating with supernuman appetite, and seemed to be in no wise possessed by the idiotic mania which young ladies have of eating only in secret, and pressing their lips together at table with a sentimental air, as if they were of a nature superior to ours. Lord Byron had not yet introduced the fashion of lack of appetite among the fair sex. So that my capricious signora abandoned herself with all her heart to the enjoyment of feasting, and in a few moments she returned to me and took a fillet of hare and a pheasant's wing from the dismantled pie. She looked at me without a smile, and said sententiously: "This east wind gives me an appetite."

"It seems that your ladyship is blessed with an excellent digestive apparatus," I observed.

"If one had not a good stomach at fifteen," she replied, "it would be as well to throw up the sponge."

"Fifteen!" I cried, looking at her closely and dropping my fork.

"Fifteen years and two months," she replied, returning to her hassock with her freshly-filled plate; "my mother is not yet thirty-two, and she married again last year. Tell me, isn't it strange that a mother should marry before her daughter? To be sure, if my darling little mother had chosen to wait for me to be married, she would have had to wait a long while. Who would ever marry a girl who, although she is beautiful, is *stupid* beyond anything one can imagine?"

There was so much merriment and good-humor in the serious air with which she made fun of me; she was such a pretty *loustig*, that tall girl with the black eyes and the long curls falling over a neck as white as alabaster; her manner of sitting on her cushion was so graceful yet so chaste in its perfect naturalness, that all my suspicion and all my evil designs vanished. I had determined to empty the decanter of wine in order to put my scruples to sleep. I pushed the decanter away, and, having satisfied my appetite, rested my elbow on the piano and began to study her anew, and under a new aspect. That revelation as to her age had thrown all my ideas into confusion. When I have desired to form an opinion concerning a person, especially one of the fair sex, I have always considered it a matter of the utmost importance to ascertain that person's age as nearly as possible. Subtlety increases so rapidly in women that six months more or less often make the difference between the innocence which is deviltry and the deviltry which is innocence. Until then I had imagined that La Grimani was at least twenty years old. She was so tall and strong and dark, and there was so much self-assurance in her glance, in her bearing, in her every movement, that everybody made the same mistake at first sight. But on examining her more closely I realized my error. Her shoulders were broad and powerful, but her breast was still undeveloped. Although her whole attitude was womanly there were certain little ways and certain expressions of the face which revealed the child. Nothing more was needed than that hearty appetite, that total absence of coquetry, and the audacious impropriety of the tête-à-tête she had arranged to have with me, to make it clear to my eyes that I had to do, not as I had supposed at first, with a proud and crafty woman of the world, but with a mischievous boarding-school girl, and I thrust aside with horror the idea of abusing her imprudence.

I remained for a long while absorbed in this scrutiny, forgetting to reply to the significant challenge I had received. She looked at me earnestly, and I no longer thought of avoiding her glance, but of analyzing it. She had the loveliest eyes in the world, flush with her face, and very wide open; their glance was always sharp and direct, and grasped its object instantly. It was imperious but not overbearing, a very rare thing in a woman. It was the revelation and the expression of a fearless, proud, and sincere mind. It questioned all things with an air of authority, and seemed to say: "Conceal nothing from me: for I have nothing to conceal from anybody."

When she saw that I did not shrink from her gaze, she was startled but not frightened; and, rising abruptly, she invited the explanation which I desired to propose.

"Signor Lelio," she said, "if you have finished your breakfast, you will kindly tell me why you came here."

"I will obey you, signora," I replied, picking up her plate and glass, which she had left on the floor, and carrying them back to the piano; "but I beg your ladyship to tell me whether the piano-tuner shall answer you sitting at the instrument, or whether the actor Lelio shall stand before you, hat in hand, ready to retire after he has had the honor to talk with you."

"Signor Lelio will kindly sit in this chair," she said, pointing to one on the right hand of the fire-place, "and I in this," she added, taking her seat on the left side, facing me and about ten feet away.

"Signora," I said, as I sat down, "in order to obey you I must go back a little. About two months ago I was playing in *Romeo and Juliet* at San Carlo. There was in one of the proscenium boxes ——"

"I can refresh your memory," interposed La Grimani. "There was in one of the proscenium boxes on the right of the stage a young woman whom you considered beautiful; but on looking at her more closely, it seemed to you that her face was so devoid of expression that you shouted to one of the ladies on the stage, loud enough to be overheard by the young woman in question ——"

"In heaven's name! signora," I interrupted, "do not repeat the words that escaped from me in my delirium, and let me tell you that I am subject to attacks of nervous irritation which make me almost insane. When I am in that condition everything offends me, everything causes me intense suffering ——"

"I do not ask why it was your pleasure to announce so concisely your judgment of the young woman in the box; I simply ask you for the rest of the story."

"In order to be perfectly truthful and coherent, I must insist upon the prologue. Under the influence of a first attack of fever, the beginning of a serious illness from which I have hardly recovered, I fancied that I could read profound contempt and frigid irony on the incomparably lovely face of the young lady in the proscenium box. I was annoyed at first, then seriously disturbed, and at last completely upset, so that I lost my head and yielded to a brutal impulse in order to put an end to the fatal spell which benumbed all my faculties and paralyzed me at the most powerful and most important part of my rôle. Your ladyship must forgive me for an act of madness; I believe in magnetism, especially on those days when I am ill and when my brain is as weak as my legs. I fancied that the young lady in the box had an injurious influence over me; and during the cruel disease which took full possession of me on the day following my offence, I will confess that she often appeared in my delirium; but always haughty, always threatening, and promising me that I should pay dearly for the blasphemy that fell from my lips. Such, signora, is the first part of my story."

I made ready my shield to ward off a volley of epigrams by way of comment on this strange tale, which, although true, was most improbable, I must confess. But the young Grimani, gazing at me with a gentleness which I had no idea could be found in conjunction with her type of beauty, said to me, leaning a little heavily on the arm of her chair:

"Your face does in truth show signs of great suffering, Signor Lelio; and if I must confess the whole truth, when I recognized you yesterday, I said to myself that I must have observed you very carelessly on the stage; for you seemed to me then ten years younger; but to-day you seem no older than you did on the stage; but still I think that you look ill, and I am very, very sorry that I caused you any irritation."

I involuntarily moved my chair nearer to hers; whereupon she at once resumed her mocking and capricious tone.

"Let us pass to the second part of your story, Signor

Lelio," she said, playing with her fan, "and be kind enough to tell me why, instead of avoiding the person the sight of whom is so hateful and prejudicial to you, you have come as far as this in pursuit of her."

"At this point the author finds himself in an embarrassing position," I replied, pushing back my chair, which moved very easily at the slightest turn in the conversation. "Shall I tell you that chance alone led me here? If I do, will your ladyship believe it? and if I say that it was not chance, will your ladyship tolerate such impertinence?"

"It matters very little to me," she rejoined, "whether it is chance, or magnetic attraction, as you will say, perhaps, that brings you to this neighborhood; I simply desire to know by what chance you became a pianotuner?"

"The chance of inspiration, signora; a pretext to obtain admission to this house was all that I wanted."

"But why did you wish to be admitted to this house?"

"I will answer frankly if your ladyship will deign first to tell me what chance induced you to admit me, although you recognized me at the first glance?"

"The chance of caprice, Signor Lelio. I was bored to death here, alone with my cousin, or with a pious old aunt whom I hardly know; and while one is hunting and the other at church, I thought that I might venture to enliven by a mad freak the ghastly solitude in which I am left to pine away."

Once more my chair of its own motion approached hers, but I hesitated to take her hand. At that moment she seemed to me decidedly forward. There are some girls who are born women, and who are corrupt before they have lost their innocence.

"She is a child, beyond doubt," I thought, "but a child

who is tired of being one, and I should be a great fool not to reply to allurements resorted to so coolly and boldly. Faith! I am sorry for the cousin! Why does he care more for hunting than for his kinswoman?"

But the signora paid no heed to the agitation that had laid hold of me. "Now the farce is at an end," she continued; "we have eaten my cousin's game and I have talked with an actor. I have fooled my aunt and my future spouse. Last week my cousin was furious because I praised you with what he considered too great warmth. Now, when he mentions you to me, and when my aunt says that the actors are all excommunicated in France, I will look at the floor with a modest and beatific expression, and laugh in my sleeve to think that I know Signor Lelio, and that I breakfasted with him, in this very room, without anyone's suspecting it. But now, Signor Lelio, you must tell me why you chose to obtain admission to this house by playing a false rôle?"

"Forgive me, signora—you just now said something which touched me deeply. You said, did you not, that you praised me last week with *great warmth?*"

"Oh! I only did it to make my cousin angry. I am not naturally enthusiastic."

When she flaunted me, it revived my zest for the adventure, and emboldened me.

"Since you are so frank with me, signora," I rejoined, "I will be equally frank with your ladyship. I sought admission to this house with the intention of atoning for my crime and humbly imploring the forgiveness of the divine beauty I blasphemed."

As I spoke, I slipped from my chair, and knelt at La Grimani's feet, and was very near taking possession of her lovely hands. She did not seem greatly moved by my action; but I saw that, to conceal a slight embarrassment, she pretended to be examining the Chinese mandarins whose gowns of purple and gold gleamed resplendent on her fan.

"Really, signor," she said, without looking at me, " you are very good to think that you owe me an apology. In the first place, if I have a stupid look, you are not at all to blame for noticing it ; in the second place, if I have not, it is a matter of absolute indifference to me whether or not you are persuaded that I have."

"I swear by all the gods, and particularly by Apollo, that I said what I did only because I was angry or mad, or it may be because of a very different sentiment, which was then but just born and was already sowing confusion in my mind. I saw that you considered me detestable, and that you were not inclined to be at all indulgent to me ; could I tranquilly resign myself to lose the only approbation which it would have been sweet and glorious for me to obtain ? In a word, signora, I am here ; I discovered your abode, and though I barely knew your name, I sought you, pursued you, and reached you in spite of distance and obstacles. I am here at your feet. Do you think that I would have surmounted such difficulties if I had not been tortured by remorse, not because of you, who justly disdain to consider the effect of your charms on a poor player like myself ; but because of God, whose fairest work I insulted and undervalued ? "

While I was speaking, I ventured to take one of her hands ; but she suddenly sprang to her feet, saying :

" Rise, signor, rise ! here is my cousin coming back from hunting."

Indeed, I had barely time to run to the piano and open it before Signor Ettore Grimani, in hunting costume and gun in hand, entered the room and deposited his wellfilled game-bag at his cousin's feet.

'Oh! don't come so near me," said the signora; "you are horribly dirty, and all those bleeding creatures make me sick. Oh! Hector, go away, I beg, and take all these nasty great dogs with you; they smell of mud and soil the floor."

The cousin was fain to be content with that outburst of gratitude, and to go to his room and perfume himself at his leisure. But he had no sooner gone out than a sort of duenna appeared and informed the signora that her aunt had returned and wished to see her.

"I will go," La Grimani replied; "and do you, signor," she said, turning to me, "take this key away with you, as it is broken, and glue it firmly. You must bring it back to-morrow, and finish replacing the missing strings. I can count on you, signor? You will be sure to come?"

"Yes, signora, you may rely upon it," I replied; and I took my leave, carrying away the wrong key, which was not broken.

I was on hand promptly on the following day. But do not think, my friends, that I was in love with that young person; the utmost that can be said is that she attracted me. She was extremely lovely; but I saw her beauty with the eyes of the body, I did not feel it through the eyes of the soul; if, from time to time, I was on the point of falling in love with that childish petulance, my doubts soon returned, and I said to myself that a girl who lied so coolly to her cousin and her governess might well have lied to me; that, perhaps, she was twenty years old or more, as I had thought at first; and that it was quite likely that she had indulged in some previous escapades for which she had been secluded in that dull villa, with no other society than a pious old woman whose duty it was to scold her, and an excellent young cousin predestined to take upon his back, in his guilelessness, all her errors, past, present and to come.

I found her in the salon with the dear cousin and three or four hunting dogs, who came very near devouring me. The signora, who was nothing if not capricious, honored those noble beasts with very different treatment from that of the day before, and although they were hardly less dirty and disagreeable, she obligingly allowed them to lie, one by one, or all in a heap, on a large sofa of red velvet with gold fringe. From time to time she sat down in the midst of them, petting some and playfully teasing others.

Before long, I concluded that this revulsion of feeling toward the dogs was a bit of affectionate coquetry addressed to her cousin; for the fair-haired Signor Ettore seemed greatly flattered by it, and I don't know which he loved best, his cousin or his dogs.

She was bewilderingly vivacious, and she seemed to be keyed up to such a high pitch, the glances that she bestowed upon me in the mirror were so keen-edged, that I longed for the cousin's departure. And he did leave the room before long. The signora gave him an errand to do. She had to ask him several times, but he finally obeyed an imperious glance, accompanied by a: "Don't you propose to go?" uttered in a tone which he seemed altogether incapable of defying.

He had no sooner disappeared than I turned away from the piano and rose, looking in the signora's eyes to see whether I should go to her or wait for her to come to me. She, too, was standing, and seemed to be trying to read in my face what I was likely to do. But she gave me little encouragement, and as I fancied that her lips were partly open to give me a harsh lesson if I should be unlucky enough to lose my wits in that perilous engagement, I began to feel somewhat disturbed inwardly. I do not know why it was that that exchange of glances, at once alluring and distrustful, that effervescence of our whole being which kept us both as motionless as statues, that alternation of audacity and fear which paralyzed me at what was perhaps the decisive moment of my adventure, and even La Grimani's black velvet gown, and the bright sunlight which shone into the room through the dark curtains and expired in a fantastic blending of light and shadow at our feet—the hour, the burning atmosphere, and the restrained beating of my heart—all combined to bring vividly to my mind an analogous scene of my youth: Signora Bianca Aldini, in the shadow of her gondola, enchaining with a magnetic glance one of my feet on the shore of the Lido, the other on the boat. I felt the same mental bewilderment, the same inward agitation, the same desire, ready to give place to the same wrath. "Can it be," I thought, "that it was self-esteem that made me desire Bianca then, or is it love that makes me desire La Grimani to-day?"

It was not possible for me to rush forth into the fields, singing recklessly, as I had on that former occasion leaped ashore on the Lido, to revenge myself for a bit of innocent coquetry. There was no other course for me to adopt than to resume my seat, no other way for me to revenge myself than to begin again on the major fifth: *A-mi-la-E-si-mi.*

I must admit that that method of venting my spite could not afford me a signal triumph. An imperceptible smile fluttered about the corners of the signora's mouth when I bent my legs to sit down, and it seemed to me that I could read these pleasant words on her face: "Lelio you are a child."—But, when I abruptly rose again, ready to hurl the piano across the room and fly to her

feet, I plainly read these terrible words in her black eye :
"Signor, you are a madman."

"Signora Aldini," I reflected, "was twenty-two years old, I was fifteen or sixteen ; now I am more than twenty-two. That Bianca should govern me absolutely was natural enough, but it is not natural that I should be made a fool of by this girl. So I must be cool."

I calmly resumed my seat, saying :

"Excuse me, signora, if I look at the clock. I cannot stay long, and this piano seems to be in sufficiently good condition for me to go about my business."

"In good condition !" she replied with unmistakable irritation. "You have put it in such good condition that I am afraid I can never play on it as long as I live. I am very angry about it. You undertook to tune it ; you must do it, Signor Lelio, for your own reputation."

"Signora," I replied, "I care no more about tuning this piano than you do about playing on it. I obeyed your command to return, in order not to compromise you by putting an end to this pretence too suddenly. But your ladyship must understand that the jest cannot be prolonged forever ; that by the third day it ceases to be amusing except to you, and that on the fourth it would be a little dangerous to me. I am neither so wealthy nor so renowned that I can afford to waste time. Will not your ladyship allow me to retire in a few moments ; then a genuine tuner will come this afternoon and finish my work, saying that I am ill and have sent him in my place. I can find a substitute who will be grateful to me for providing him with a new customer, all without betraying our little secret, and without making myself known."

The signora did not say a word in reply ; but she turned as pale as death, and again I felt that I was beaten. The cousin returned. I could not restrain a gesture of annoyance. The signora noticed it, and again she triumphed; and again, seeing that I did not propose to go, she amused herself by playing upon my inward agitation.

She became very rosy and animated once more. She plied her cousin with cajoleries which were so close to the line between affection and irony that soon neither he nor I knew what to think. Then she suddenly turned her back on him, and, coming to my side, requested me, in a low tone and with a mysterious air, to keep the piano a quarter of a tone below the pitch, because she had a contralto voice. Whom was she trying to impose upon—her cousin or myself—by telling me that great secret as if it were a matter of such importance? I was on the point of going up to Hector and shaking hands with him, for we seemed to me to cut an equally foolish and laughable figure. But I saw that the excellent youth attached more importance to the matter than I did, and he cast a sidelong glance at me with such a profound and crafty expression, that I had much difficulty in refraining from laughter. I answered La Grimani, under my breath and with a still more confidential air:

"I have anticipated your wishes, signora, and the piano is just in tune with the orchestra at San Carlo, where they lowered the pitch last season because of my cold."

Thereupon, the signora took her cousin's arm with a theatrical gesture, and hurriedly led him into the garden. As they walked back and forth in front of the house, and I could see their shadows on the curtain, I took my stand behind the curtain and listened to their conversation.

"That is exactly what I wanted to say to you, my dear cousin," the signora was saying. "This man has a strange, terrifying face; he has no idea what a piano is, and he will never finish tuning it. You will see! He is a mere adventurer, mark my words. We must keep our eyes on him, and do you hold your watch in your hand when he comes near you. I would take my oath that when I leaned over the piano, unsuspectingly, to tell him to lower the pitch, he put out his hand to steal my gold chain."

"Nonsense! you are joking, cousin! It is impossible that a thief should be so bold. That isn't what I want to say to you at all, and you pretend not to understand me."

"I pretend, Hector? You accuse me of pretending? I pretend! Come, tell me if you really think you are worth the trouble it would give me to make up a falsehood?"

"This severity is quite useless, cousin. It seems at all events that I am worth the trouble of seeking an opportunity to make humiliating speeches to me."

"But what are you talking about, I would ask, cousin? And why do you say that this man ——"

"I say that this man is not a piano-tuner, that he is not tuning your piano, that he never tuned a piano in his life. I say that he never takes his eye off you, that he watches your every movement, that he breathes in every word you speak. I say that he must have seen you somewhere, at Naples or Florence, at the theatre or driving, and that he fell in love with you."

"And gained admittance here, *in disguise*, to see me, and perhaps to seduce me, the scoundrel, the villain!"

Having said thus much with great vehemence, the signora threw herself back on a bench, laughing uproariously. As I saw the cousin stalking toward the door of the salon, apparently in a furious passion, I returned to my post, and, arming myself with my tuning hammer, resolved to strike him down with it if he should attempt to insult me; for I had already set him down as one of the men who arrange matters so as to avoid fighting, and who call their servants when one challenges them within hearing of the antechamber.

"He will fall dead before he pulls that bell-rope," I thought, as I grasped the hammer and cast a rapid glance about me. But my adventure did not long retain this dramatic aspect. I saw the signora and her cousin, arm-in-arm once more, walking on the terrace, and pausing from time to time at the half-open glass door to look at me, she with a mocking, he with an embarrassed air. I no longer knew what they were saying to each other, and my wrath rose higher and higher in my throat.

Suddenly a pretty soubrette joined them on the terrace. The signora spoke to her with much animation, now laughing, now assuming an imperious tone. The soubrette seemed to hesitate; the cousin seemed to be urging the signora to do nothing extravagant. At last the maid came to me in some confusion, and said, blushing to the roots of her hair:

"Signor, the signora bids me say to you, in so many words, that you are an insolent person, and that you would do much better to tune the piano than to stare at her as you are doing. Pardon me, signor. I am very sure that it is a jest."

"And I take it as such," I replied; "but say to the signora that I present my profound respects to her, and that I beg her not to think me insolent enough to stare at her. I was not so much as thinking of her, and if I must tell you the truth, it was you, my lovely maid, whom I saw out in the field, and who engrossed me so that I forgot to go on with my work."

"I, signor," said the soubrette, blushing more hotly

than ever, and hanging her head in her embarrassment.
" How could I engross the signor ? "

" Because you are a hundred times prettier than your mistress," I said, putting my arm about her and giving her a kiss before she had time to suspect my purpose.

She was a pretty village girl, the signora's foster sister. She too was dark and tall and slender, but timid in her manner, and as artless and gentle in her bearing as her young mistress was cunning and determined. She was thrown into such confusion by being embraced so unceremoniously before the signora, who had come to the door of the salon, followed by her idiotic cousin, that she fled, hiding her face in her blue apron with silver border. The signora, who was equally surprised to find that I took her impertinence so philosophically, stepped back, and the cousin, who had seen nothing, repeated several times the question : "What is it ? What's the matter ? "

The poor girl would not pause in her flight to reply, and the signora laughed a forced laugh which I pretended not to notice.

A few moments later she reappeared alone. Her face wore an expression which was meant to be severe, but was really confused and distressed.

"It is lucky for us both, signor," she said in a voice that trembled slightly, "that my cousin is simple-minded and gullible; for you must know that he is of a jealous and quarrelsome disposition."

"Really, signora ? " I replied, gravely.

"Do not laugh at me, signor," she retorted angrily. "One may be easily deceived when one loves ; but the name of Grimani stands for personal courage."

"I do not doubt it, signora," I replied in the same tone.

"I beg you, therefore, signor," she continued, still

speaking with involuntary vehemence, "not to come here again; for all this jesting might end badly."

"That is as you please, signora," I replied, as imperturbably as before.

"It is evident, however, signor, that you find it very amusing; for you do not seem disposed to put an end to it."

"If I amuse myself, signora, it is by way of being obedient, as we all amuse ourselves in Italy under the reign of Napoleon the Great. I wished to retire an hour ago, and it was you who forbade it."

"I forbade it? Do you dare to say that I forbade it?"

"I intended to say, signora, that you did not think of it; for I expected that you would give me some sort of a plausible pretext for taking my leave in the midst of my task; and, for my own part, it was impossible for me to imagine such a pretext. It would be so entirely unnatural in the present condition of the piano, and I am so firmly resolved to do nothing that can possibly compromise you, that I will return to-morrow."

"You will do nothing of the kind."

"I beg your ladyship's pardon, I will return to-morrow."

"For what purpose, signor? And by what right?"

"I will return to gratify Signor Ettore's curiosity, for he is very much puzzled to know who I am; and I will return because you have yourself given me the right to face the man with whom you were pleased to make merry at my expense."

"Is that a threat, Signor Lelio?" she asked, concealing her fright beneath the cloak of pride.

"No, signora. A man who does not falter before another man is not of the threatening sort."

"But my cousin said nothing to you, signor; I did all this jesting against his will."

"But he is jealous and quarrelsome. Moreover, he is brave. Now, I am not jealous, signora, I have neither the right nor the desire to be. But I am quarrelsome, and it may be too that, although my name is not Grimani, I am a brave man; what do you know about it?"

"Oh! I have no doubt of it, Lelio!" she cried, in a tone that made me quiver from head to foot, it was so entirely different from what I had been hearing for two or three days.

I looked at her in amazement; she lowered her eyes with an air at once modest and proud. Once again I was disarmed.

"Signora," I said, "I will do whatever you choose, as you choose, and nothing that you do not choose."

She hesitated a moment.

"You cannot come again as a piano-tuner," said she; "if you do, you will compromise me, for my cousin will certainly tell my aunt that he suspects you of being a libertine in search of adventures; and, when my aunt hears it, she will tell my mother. And let me tell you Signor Lelio, that there is only one person in the world for whom I care in the least, and that is my mother; that there is only one thing in the world that I dread, and that is my mother's displeasure. And yet she brought me up very badly, as you see; she spoiled me shockingly; but she is so dear, so sweet, so loving, so sad— She loves me so dearly—if you only knew!"

A great tear glistened in the signora's black eye; she tried for some time to hold it back, but at last it fell on her hand. Deeply moved, assailed and overthrown by the formidable little god with whom one cannot afford to trifle, I put my lips to that lovely hand and greedily drank that sweet tear, a subtle poison which kindled a flame in my bosom. I heard the cousin returning, and, rising hurriedly, I said:

"*Addio,* signora, I will obey you blindly, I swear upon my honor; if your cousin insults me, I will swallow his insults; I will play a coward's part rather than cause you to shed a second tear."

With that I bowed to the ground and left the room. The cousin did not seem to me so bellicose as she had depicted him; for he saluted me first when I passed him. I walked slowly from the house, depressed beyond words; for I was in love, and I must not return. On becoming sincere, my love became generous.

I turned several times to catch a glimpse of the signora's velvet dress, but she had disappeared. As I was passing through the gate of the park, I saw her in a narrow path which followed the wall on the inside. She had run, in order to reach that point as soon as I did, and when I spied her she strove to assume a slow and pensive gait; but she was all out of breath and her lovely black hair was disarranged by the branches she had hurriedly thrust aside as she ran through the underbrush. I started to join her, but she made a sign to indicate that somebody was following her. I tried to pass through the gate, but I could not make up my mind to do it. Thereupon, she waved her hand to bid me farewell, accompanying the gesture with an unutterable glance and smile. At that moment she was more beautiful than I had ever seen her. I placed one hand on my heart, the other on my forehead, and hurried away, mad with joy and love. I had seen the branches moving just behind the signora; but, there as elsewhere, the cousin arrived too late. I had disappeared.

I found in my room a letter from Checchina. "I had

started to join you," she wrote, "and to rest a while from the fatigues of the stage in the pleasant shade of Cafaggiolo. I was upset at San Giovanni; I have nothing worse than a few bruises, but my carriage is broken. The bungling workmen in this village say they must have three days to repair it. Take your calèche and come and fetch me, unless you wish me to die of ennui in this muleteers' tavern."

I set out an hour later and reached San Giovanni at daybreak.

"How does it happen that you are alone?" I asked, trying to escape from her long arms and her sisterly embraces, which had become unendurable to me since my illness, because of the perfumes with which she saturated herself beyond all reason, whether because she fancied that she was imitating the great ladies, or because she loved passionately anything that appeals to the senses.

"I have had a row with Nasi," she said; "I have left him, and I don't want to hear any more about him!"

"It can't be very serious," I replied, "as you are on your way to take up your quarters in his house."

"On the contrary, it is very serious; for I have forbidden him to follow me."

"And apparently you intended to deprive him of the means of doing so, when you took his carriage to run away in, and broke it on the road."

"It's his own fault, for I had to keep urging the postilions. Why has he adopted the bad habit of following me? I would have liked to be killed by the accident, and have him arrive in time to see me die, and to learn what it is to thwart a woman like me."

"That is to say, a mad woman. But you will not have the pleasure of dying for revenge, in the first place, because you are not hurt, and secondly, because he has not run after you."

"Oh! he probably passed through here last night without suspecting that I was here, and you must have met him on your way. We will go and join him at Cafaggiolo."

"He is just crazy enough for that."

"If I were perfectly sure of it, I would like to remain here in hiding a week, just to worry him and make him think that I have gone to France, as I threatened to do."

"As you please, my dear: I salute you and leave my carriage at your service. For my own part, I have little liking for this region and this inn."

"If you were not a dolt, you would avenge me, Lelio!"

"Thanks! I have not been insulted; nor you either, I fancy."

"Oh! I have been mortally insulted, Lelio!"

"I suppose he refused to give you twenty thousand francs' worth of white gloves, and insisted on giving you diamonds worth fifty thousand instead; something like that, no doubt?"

"No, no, Lelio; he wants to marry!"

"Provided that he doesn't want to marry you, that is a most pardonable desire."

"And the most horrible part of it is that he had an idea that he could induce me to consent to his marriage and still retain my good graces. After such an insult, would you believe that he had the audacity to offer me a million, on condition that I would allow him to marry, and that I would remain faithful to him!"

"A million! the devil! that is at least the fortieth million I have known of you refusing, my poor Checchina.

The millions you have spurned would be enough to keep the whole royal family!"

"You are always joking, Lelio. The day will come when you will see that, if I had chosen, I might have been a queen like some other women. Are Napoleon's sisters any more beautiful than I am? Have they more talent, more wit, more spirit? Ah! how well I could manage a kingdom!"

"Almost as well as you could keep books by double entry in a business house. Upon my word! you have put on your wrapper wrong side before, and you are wiping tears from your lovely eyes with one of your silk stockings. Put aside these ambitious dreams for a moment, dress yourself, and let us be off."

As we returned to the villa at Cafaggiolo, by dint of allowing my travelling companion to give a free rein to her heroic declamations, her digressions and her boasting, I succeeded, not without difficulty, in finding out that honest Nasi had been fascinated at a ball by a lovely young person, and had asked her hand in marriage; that he had gone to Checchina to inform her of his determination; that, as she had adopted the expedient of fainting and going into convulsions, he had been so dismayed by the violence of her despair, that he had begged her to consent to a middle course and to remain his mistress in spite of his marriage. Thereupon Checchina, seeing that he was weakening, had haughtily refused to share her lover's heart and purse. She had ordered posthorses, and had signed, or pretended to sign, an engagement with the Opera at Paris. The easy-going Nasi had been unable to endure the thought of giving up a woman whom he was not sure that he had ceased to adore, for a woman whom he was not sure that he had begun to adore. He had begged the singer's forgiveness; he had retracted his offer of marriage, and had ceased his attentions to the illustrious beauty, whose name Checchina did not know. Checchina had allowed herself to be prevailed upon; but she had learned indirectly, on the day following this great sacrifice, that Nasi was entitled to no great credit therefor, inasmuch as, between the scene of frenzied despair and the reconciliation, his offer of marriage had been rejected, and he had been cast aside in favor of a happy rival. Checchina, wounded to the quick, had left Naples, leaving a withering letter for the count, in which she declared that she would never see him again; and, taking the road to France—for all roads lead to Paris as well as to Rome—she hastened to Cafaggiolo to wait until her lover should come in pursuit of her, and place his body across her path to prevent her from proceeding farther with a vengeance of which she was beginning to be a little weary.

All this was not mere vulgar and avaricious scheming on Checchina's part. She loved opulence, it is true, and could not do without it; but she had such implicit faith in her destiny, and was naturally so audacious, that she constantly risked the good fortune of one day for that of the morrow. She passed the Rubicon every morning, confident of finding on the other bank a more flourishing realm than the one she left behind. Thus there was nothing base and low-minded in this feminine trickery, because there was in it no element of fear. She did not play at grief; she made neither false promises nor hypocritical prayers. In her moments of vexation she had genuine paroxysms of nervous excitement. Why were her lovers so credulous as to mistake the vehemence of her anger for the result of profound grief resisted by pride? Is it not our own fault when we are duped by our own vanity?

Moreover, even if Checchina did play a bit at tragedy in her boudoir, in order to preserve her empire, she had an ample excuse in the absolute sincerity of her conduct. I have never known a woman more fearlessly frank, more faithful to lovers who were faithful to her, more reckless in her admissions when she revenged herself in kind, more incapable of recovering her power by means of a falsehood. To be sure her love was not strong enough for that, and no man seemed to her to be worth the trouble of putting constraint upon herself and of humiliating herself in her own eyes by prolonged dissembling. I have often thought that women are very foolish to demand so much frankness when we are so far from appreciating the merit of fidelity. I have often learned by my own experience that one must have more passion to carry out a falsehood, than courage to tell the truth. It is so easy to be sincere with persons one does not love! It is so pleasant to be sincere with those whom one has ceased to love!

This simple reflection will explain why it was impossible for me to love Checchina for long, and also why it was impossible for me not to esteem her always, despite her insolent outbreaks and her immeasurable ambition. I soon found out that she was a detestable mistress and an excellent friend; and then, too, there was a sort of poetic charm in that adventuress-like energy, in that disregard for wealth inspired by the very love of wealth, in that incredible conceit, always crowned by even more incredible success. She was forever comparing herself favorably to Napoleon's sisters, and making herself out the equal of Napoleon himself. That was amusing and not too ridiculous. In her own sphere she was as bold and as fortunate as the great conqueror. She never had for lovers any but young, handsome, rich and honorable men; and I do not believe that a single one of them ever complained of her after leaving or losing her; for in reality she had a great and noble heart. She could always atone for a thousand foolish and mischievous exploits by one decisive display of strength of character and kindness of heart. In a word, she was brave, both morally and physically, and people of that temperament are always good for something, wherever they may be and whatever they may do.

"My poor child," I said to her as we drove along, "you will be nicely caught if Nasi takes you at your word and lets you start for France."

"There's no danger of that," she said with a smile, forgetting that she had just told me that she would not for anything in the world allow herself to be softened by his submission.

"But suppose that does happen, what will you do? You have nothing in the world, and you are not in the habit of keeping the gifts of your lovers when you part. That is what makes me esteem you a little bit, despite all your faults. Come, tell me, what is going to become of you?"

"I shall be very sorry," she replied; "yes, really, Lelio, I shall regret it; for Nasi is an excellent fellow, he has a big heart. I will bet that I shall weep for—I don't know how long! But after all, one either has a destiny or one hasn't. If it is God's will that I go to France, it would seem to be because I am likely to have no more luck in Italy. If I am parted from that dear, affectionate lover of mine, I have no doubt that it is because a more devoted and more courageous man is waiting yonder for me, to marry me, and prove to the world that love is superior to all prejudices. Mark my words, Lelio, I shall be a princess, perhaps a queen. An old fortune-teller of Malamocco predicted it in my horoscope when I was only four years old, and I have always believed it: a proof that it must be so!"

"A conclusive proof," I rejoined, "an unanswerable argument! Queen of Barataria, I salute you!"

"What is Barataria? Is it Cimarosa's new opera?"

"No, it is the name of the star that presides over your destiny."

We arrived at Cafaggiolo and did not find Nasi there.

"Your star is waning, fortune is abandoning you," I said to the girl from Chioggia.

She bit her lips and replied at once, with a smile:

"There is always a mist on the lagoons before sunrise. In any event we must keep up our strength and so be prepared for the blows of destiny."

As she spoke, she took her seat at the table and ate almost the whole of a pope's eye stuffed with truffles; after which she slept twelve hours without a break, passed three hours at her toilet, and sparkled with wit and nonsense until evening. Nasi did not appear.

For my own part, amid the merriment and animation which that excellent girl had brought into my solitude, I was absorbed by the memory of my adventure at the Grimani villa, and tortured by the longing to see my fair patrician once more. But how was I to do it? I cudgelled my brain to no purpose to invent some means which would not compromise her. When I left her I had sworn to do nothing imprudent. As I reviewed in my mind my impressions of those last moments, when she had appeared in such an artless and touching aspect, I felt that I could not act inconsiderately with respect to her without forfeiting my own esteem. I dared not make inquiries concerning her friends, still less concerning her domestic arrangements. I had refrained from making acquaintances in the neighborhood, and now I almost regretted that I had done so; for I might have learned by accident what I dared not ask directly. The servant who waited upon me was a Neapolitan who had come with me, and, like myself, had never been in that region before. The gardener was stupid and deaf. An old care-taker, in charge of the villa since Nasi's childhood, might perhaps have enlightened me; but I was afraid to question her, for she was inquisitive and loquacious. She was much disturbed to know where I went; and, during the three days that I had failed to bring her any game or to give an account of my rambles, she was so wrought up that I trembled lest she should discover my romance. The bare mention of a name might put her on the track. So I was very careful not to pronounce it. I did not wish to go to Florence; I was too well known there; if I showed my face there, I was certain to be overwhelmed with visits. The unhealthy and misanthropical frame of mind which had caused me to seek the solitude of Cafaggiolo, had led me likewise to conceal my name and profession from the very servants in the house as well as from the neighbors. It was necessary now for me to guard my *incognito* more closely than ever; for I supposed that the count would soon arrive, and that his fancy for marriage would lead him to desire to bury in mystery Checchina's presence in his house.

Two days passed with no word from Nasi, who might have enlightened me; and I had not ventured to take a step out-of-doors. Checchina had a heavy cold and considerable pain, as a result of the mishaps of her journey. It may well be that, as she did not quite know what course to adopt with me, and as she preferred not to seem to be waiting for her faithless lover, after swearing that she would not wait for him, she was not sorry to have a valid excuse for remaining at Cafaggiolo. One morning, finding that I could not stand it any longer, for that signorina of fifteen with her little white hands and great black eyes was always in my head, I took my game-bag, called my dog, and started out to hunt, forgetting nothing but my rifle. In vain did I prowl about the Grimani villa; I did not see a living being, I did not hear a human sound. All the gates of the park were locked, and I noticed that on the main avenue, at the end of which one could catch a glimpse of the house-front, some large trees had been felled and their dense foliage completely intercepted the view. Had that barricade been erected with premeditation ? Was it an act of revenge on the cousin's part ? Was it a precaution taken by the aunt ? Was it a mischievous exploit of my heroine herself ? "If I thought that!" I said to myself. But I did not think it. I much preferred to suppose that she was lamenting over my absence and her own captivity, and I formed innumerable plans to set her free, each more absurd than the last.

On returning to Cafaggiolo, I found in Checchina's bedroom a pretty village maiden whom I at once recognized as La Grimani's foster sister.

"Here's a lovely child who refuses to give her message to anybody but you, Lelio," said Checchina, who had seated her unceremoniously on the side of her bed. "I have taken her under my protection because old Catalina insisted on sending her away with an insolent answer. But I saw by her modest manner that she is a good girl, and I haven't asked her any injudicious questions. Isn't that true, my pretty brunette ? Come, don't be shamefaced, but go into the salon with Signor Lelio. I am not inquisitive, I tell you ; I have something else to do besides annoy my friends."

" Come, my dear child," I said to the soubrette, "and have no fear; you have only honorable people to deal with here."

The poor girl stood in the middle of the floor, bewildered, and in such distress that it made one's heart ache. Although she had had the courage to conceal the object of her visit up to that time, she took from her pocket, in her confusion, and half revealed a note which she instantly thrust out of sight again, distracted between her fears for her own honor and for her mistress's.

"Oh dear !" she said at last in a trembling voice, "suppose the signora should think that I came here with any evil intention ! "

"My poor child, I think nothing at all," replied kindhearted Checchina, opening a book and reading it with eye-glasses, although her sight was excellent; for she thought that it was good form to have weak eyes.

" The signora is so kind and received me with so much confidence," continued the girl.

"Your appearance must inspire confidence in everybody," replied the singer, "and if I am kind to you, it is because you deserve it. Come, come ; I am not inquisitive, I tell you ; say what you have to say to Signor Lelio, it will not vex me in the slightest degree. Come, take her away, Lelio ! Poor child ! she thinks she is ruined. Nonsense, my dear, actors are just as honorable as other people, be sure of that."

The girl made a low courtesy and followed me into the salon. Her heart was beating as if it would break the lacings of her green velvet waist, and her cheeks were as scarlet as her skirt. She hastily took the letter from her pocket and, after handing it to me, stepped back, she was so afraid that I would be as rude to her as I was before. I reassured her by the tranquillity of my demeanor, and asked her if she had anything more to say to me.

"I am to wait for the answer," she replied, with an air of the most profound distress.

"Very well," said I, "go and wait in the signora's apartment."

And I escorted her back to Checchina.

"This excellent girl," I explained, "wishes to enter the services of a lady in Florence whom I know very well, and she has come to me for a letter of recommendation. Will you allow her to stay with you while I go and write it?"

"Yes, yes, to be sure!" replied Checchina, motioning her to sit down, and smiling at her with an amiable and patronizing air. This sweetness and simplicity of manner toward persons of her former station in life were among the Chioggian's excellent qualities. While she mimicked the affectations of the great lady, she retained the brusque and ingenuous kindliness of the fisherman's child. Her manners, though often ridiculous, were always affable; and if she did enjoy lying in state under a satin coverlet trimmed with lace, for the benefit of that poor village girl, she found none the less, in her heart and on her lips, affectionate words to encourage her in her humility.

The signora's letter was in these words:

"Three days without coming again! Either you have little wit, or you have little desire to see me again. Is it for me to find a way of continuing our friendly relations? If you have not tried to find one, you are a fool; if you have tried and failed, you are what you accuse me of being. To prove that I am neither *haughty* nor *stupid*, I write to make an appointment with you. To-morrow,

Sunday, morning I shall be at eight o'clock mass, at *Santa Maria del Sasso,* Florence. My aunt is ill ; only Lila, my foster sister, will accompany me. If the footman or coachman notice you or question you, give them money ; they are rascals. *Addio,* until to-morrow."

To reply, to promise, to swear, to express my thanks, and to hand to Lila the most bombastic of love-letters, was an affair of a few moments only. But when I attempted to slip a gold piece into the messenger's hand, I was checked by a glance instinct with melancholy dignity. From pure devotion to her mistress she had yielded to her caprice ; but it was evident that her conscience reproached her for that weakness, and that to offer to pay her for it would have been to punish and mortify her cruelly. At that moment I reproached myself bitterly for the kiss I had ventured to steal from her, in order to pique her mistress, and I tried to atone for my fault by escorting her to the end of the garden with as much respect and courtesy as I could have shown to any great lady.

I was very nervous all the rest of the day. Checchina noticed my preoccupation.

"Come, Lelio," she said, toward the close of the supper which we ate together on a pretty little terrace shaded by grape-vines and jasmine ; "I see that you are worried about something ; why not open your heart to me ? Did I ever betray a secret ? Am I not worthy of your confidence ? Have I deserved to have you withdraw it from me ? "

"No, my dear Checchina," I replied, "I appreciate your discretion "—and it is certain that she would have kept Brutus's secrets as well as ever Portia did ;—" but," I added, " even if all my secrets belong to you, there are others——"

"I know what you are going to say," she exclaimed. "That there are others which don't belong to you alone, and which you have no right to betray; but if I guess them in spite of you, ought you to carry your scruples so far as to deny, all to no purpose, what I know as well as you do? You know, my friend, I understand that pretty girl's call perfectly well; I saw her hand in her pocket, and before she had said good-morning to me, I knew that she had brought a letter. The timid and distressed air of that poor Iris "—Checchina had been very fond of mythological references ever since she had spelled out Tasso's *Aminta* and Guarini's *Adone*—" told me plainly enough that there was a genuine romance behind it, a great lady afraid of public opinion, or a young damsel risking her future union with some worthy citizen. One thing is certain, that you have made one of those conquests of which you men are so proud, because they are supposed to be difficult and require a lot of mystery. You see that I have guessed the secret, don't you?"

I answered with a smile.

"I won't ask you any more questions," she continued; "I know that you are not likely to confide the person's name, nor her rank, nor her place of abode to me; indeed, those things don't interest me. But I may ask you whether you are in raptures or in despair, and you must tell me if I can be of any use to you."

"If I need you, I will tell you so," I replied; "and as for telling you whether I am in raptures or in despair, I can assure you that I am in neither as yet."

"Very good! very good! beware of one no less than of the other; for, in either case, there's no occasion for such great excitement."

"What do you know about it?"

"My dear Lelio," she replied in a sententious tone,

"let us suppose that you are in raptures. What is one yielding woman more or less in the life of a man of the stage: of the stage, where the women are so beautiful and so sparkling with wit? Do you propose to lose your head over a conquest in aristocratic society? Vanity! mere vanity! Society women are as inferior to us in every respect as vanity is to glory."

"That is true modesty, and I congratulate you," I replied; "but might we not give the aphorism another turn, and say that it is vanity, not love, which brings society men to the feet of actresses?"

"Oh! but what a difference there is!" cried Checchina. "A great and beautiful actress is a creature privileged by nature and exalted by the prestige of art; exposed to the eyes of men in all the splendor of her beauty, her talent and her renown, is it not natural that she should arouse admiration and kindle desire? Why, then, should you actors, who triumph over the great majority of us before the great nobles do; you, who marry us when we are inclined to settle down, and who assert your rights over us when we have passionate hearts; you, who allow others to play the rôle of magnificent lovers and who are always the preferred lovers, or at all events the friends of our hearts—why should you turn your thoughts toward these patrician women who smile at you with their lips only, and applaud you with the tips of their fingers? Ah! Lelio, Lelio! I am afraid that in this instance your good sense has gone astray in some idiotic adventure. If I were in your place, rather than be flattered by the ogling of some middle-aged marchioness, I would turn my attention to some pretty chorus-girl, La Torquata, or La Gargani. Yes! yes!" she cried, becoming more earnest as she saw me smiling; "such girls as those are apparently more forward, but I maintain that they are in reality less corrupt than your salon Cidalisas. You would not be obliged to play a long sentimental comedy with them, or engage in a wretched contest of bright sayings. But that's just like you men! The crest on a carriage, the livery of a footman, those are enough to embellish in your eyes the first titled harridan who bestows a patronizing glance on you."

"My dear friend," I replied, "all that you say is most sensible; but your argument is weak in that it is not based upon a single fact. For my honor's sake, you might, I think, have assumed that old age and ugliness are not indispensable qualities in any patrician who falls in love with me. There have been some who were young and lovely who have had eyes in their heads, and since you compel me to say absurd things in absurd language, in order to close your mouth, let me tell you that the object of my *flame* is fifteen years old, and that she is as beautiful as the goddess *Cypris* whose exploits you learn by heart in *bouts-rimés*."

"Lelio!" cried Checchina, laughing heartily, "you are the most insufferable coxcomb that I ever met."

"If I am a coxcomb, fair princess," I cried, "you are somewhat to blame for it, so people say."

"Very well," said she, "if you are telling the truth, if your mistress, by reason of her beauty, deserves the follies you are about to commit for her, beware of one thing, and that is that you do not find yourself in the depths of despair within a week."

"What in the deuce is the matter to-day, Signora Checchina, that you say such disagreeable things to me?"

"Let us not joke any more," she said, putting her hand on mine with a friendly gesture. "I know you better than you know yourself. You are seriously in love, and you are going to suffer—"

"Nonsense, nonsense! in your old age, Checca, you can retire to Malamocco and tell fortunes for the boatmen on the lagoons; meanwhile, my fair sorceress, allow me to go to meet my fortune without cowardly presentiments."

"No! no! I will not be quiet until I have drawn your horoscope. If it were a question of a woman who is suited to you, I should not think of vexing you; but a woman of noble birth, a society woman, a marchioness or a woman of the middle class, I don't care which it may be—I hate them all! When I see that idiot Nasi throw me aside for a creature who doesn't come up to my knees, I will stake my head, why, I say to myself that all men are vain and foolish. And so I predict that you will not be loved, because a society woman cannot love an actor; and if by any chance you are loved, you will be all the more miserable; for you will be humiliated."

"Humiliated! What do you mean by that, Checchina?"

"By what do you recognize love, Lelio? by the pleasure you give or the pleasure you receive?"

"By both, of course! What are you driving at?"

"Is it not the same with devotion as with pleasure? Must it not be mutual?"

"To be sure; what then?"

"How much devotion do you expect to find in your mistress? a few nights of pleasure? You seem at a loss to reply."

"I am, in truth; I told you that she is fifteen years old, and I am an honorable man."

"Do you hope to marry her?"

"I, marry a rich girl of a noble family? God forbid! In heaven's name, do you think that I am consumed with matrimoniomania, as you are?"

"Why, I suppose that you desire to marry her; do you think that she will consent? are you sure of it?"

"But I will tell you that I wouldn't marry anyone, on any consideration."

"If that is because your suit would be ill received, your rôle is a very pitiful one, my dear Lelio!"

"*Corpo di Bacco!* you bore me, Checchina!"

"That is my purpose, dear friend of my heart. Now, then, you do not think of marrying, because that would be impertinent presumption on your part, and you are a man of spirit. You do not think of seduction, because that would be a crime, and you are a man of heart. Tell me, is your romance likely to be very amusing?"

"Why, you dense, matter-of-fact creature, you know nothing whatever about sentiment. If I choose to indulge in a pastoral idyll, who will prevent me?"

"That is very pretty in music; in love it must be decidedly dull."

"But it is neither criminal nor humiliating."

"Then why are you so excited? Why are you so sad, Lelio?"

"You are dreaming, Checchina; I am as placid and light-hearted as usual. Let us have no more of these empty words; I do not ask you to be silent about the little I have told you, for I have confidence in you. To reassure you concerning my frame of mind, let me tell you this one thing: I am more proud of my profession of actor than ever nobleman was of his marquisate. Nobody on earth has the power to make me blush. Whatever you may say, I shall never be conceited enough to aspire to extraordinary devotion, and if a spark of love warms my heart at this moment, the modest joy of inspiring a little love is sufficient for me. I do not deny the numerous superiorities of actresses over society women. There is more beauty, grace, wit and fire in the wings than elsewhere, I know. There is no more modesty, unselfishness, chastity and loyalty among great ladies than elsewhere; that, too, I know. But youth and beauty are idols which make us bend the knee everywhere; and as for the prejudices of rank, it is a good deal for a woman brought up under tyrannical laws to bestow in secret one poor glance, one poor heart-throb upon a man whom her prejudices forbid her to look upon as a being of her own species. That poor glance, that poor palpitation, would be a mere trifle to the unbounded desire born of a great passion; but as I have told you, cousin, I have not got to that point."

"But how do you know that you won't come to it?"

"When I do, it will be time enough to preach to me."

"It will be too late; you will suffer!"

"Ah! Cassandra, I prithee let me love on!"

At seven o'clock the next morning I was wandering slowly about in the shadow of the pillars of Santa Maria. That assignation was the very greatest piece of imprudence that my young signora could commit, for my face was as well known to most of the people of Florence as the ground under their horses' feet. So I took the most minute precautions, entering the city by the uncertain light of dawn, keeping out of sight in the chapels, with my face buried in my cloak, gliding along noiselessly, taking care not to disturb by the slightest sound the faithful at prayer, among whom I tried to discover the lady of my thoughts. I did not wait long; pretty Lila appeared from behind a pillar, and indicated by her glance an empty confessional, whose mysterious recess would hold two people. In the girl's quick and intelligent glance there was a touch of sadness which went to my heart. I knelt in the confessional, a few moments later, a dark shadow glided in and knelt beside me. Lila bent over a chair, between us and the congregation, who, luckily, were engrossed at that moment by the beginning of the mass, and falling noiselessly on their knees to the tones of the bell of the *introit*.

The signora was enveloped in a long black veil, and she held it over her face with her hands for a few seconds. She did not speak to me, but bent her lovely head as if she had come to the church to pray; but, despite all her efforts to appear calm, I saw that her breast was heaving, and that, in the midst of her audacity, she was terror-stricken. I dared not encourage her with loving words, for I knew how quick she was at sarcastic repartee, and I could not be sure what tone she would take with me under those delicate circumstances. I realized simply this, that the more she exposed herself with me, the more respectful and submissive my attitude must be. With such a nature as hers, presumption would have been speedily repelled by scorn. At last I understood that I must break the silence, and I thanked her awkwardly enough for the favor of that meeting. My timidity seemed to restore her courage. She softly raised a corner of her veil, rested her arm with less constraint on the rail of the confessional, and said to me in a half-mocking, half-melting tone:

"For what do you thank me, please?"

"For relying upon my obedience, signora," I replied; "for not doubting the eagerness with which I would come to receive your orders."

"I understand then," she retorted—and her tone was altogether jocular—"that your presence here is an act of pure obedience?"

"I should not dare to take the liberty to have any thoughts concerning the present situation, except that I am your slave, and that, having a sovereign command to lay upon me, you bade me come and kneel here."

"You are a man of the most perfect breeding," she replied, slowly unfolding her fan in front of her face, and pulling up her black mitt over her beautifully moulded arm with as much ease of manner as if she were speaking to her cousin.

She continued in that strain, and in a very few moments I was bewildered and almost saddened by her strange and captious chatter.

"What is the use," I said to myself, "of so much audacity for so little love ? An assignation in a church, in plain sight of a whole congregation, the danger of being discovered, cursed and disowned by her whole family and her whole caste—all for the sake of exchanging jokes with me, as she might with a friend of her own sex in her box at the theatre ! Does she delight in adventures from pure love of danger ? If she takes such risks without loving me, what will she do for the man she does love ? And then, how do I know how many times and for whom she has already exposed herself in the same way ? If she has never done it, it is only because she has never had the opportunity. She is so young ! But what an endless series of gallant adventures the perilous future has in store for her, and how many men will abuse their opportunities, and how many stains will mar this lovely flower, so intensely eager to bloom in the wind of passion !"

She noticed my preoccupation, and said to me, in a sharp tone :

"You look as if you were bored ? "

I was about to reply when a slight sound made us both turn our heads involuntarily. The wooden shutter which covers the grated window through which the priest receives confessions opened behind us, and a yellow, wrinkled face, with a stern and penetrating glance, appeared in the opening like a bad dream. I hastily turned away before that unwelcome intruder had time to examine my features. But I dared not go away, for fear of attracting the attention of those roundabout. Thereupon I heard these words addressed to my confederate:

"Signora, the person beside you did not come to the Lord's house to listen to the sacred service. I have seen by his entire attitude and by the distraction it has caused you, that the church is being profaned by an illicit conversation. Order this person to retire or I shall be compelled to inform the signora, your aunt, with how little fervor you listen to the blessed mass, and how willingly you open your ears to the empty words of young men who steal to a place by your side."

The shutter was instantly closed, and we remained for some seconds absolutely motionless, afraid of betraying ourselves by the slightest movement. Then Lila came nearer to us and whispered to her mistress:

"For heaven's sake, let us go, signora! Abbé Cignola, who has been prowling about the church for a quarter of an hour, just went into the confessional and came out again almost immediately, after looking at you through the window, I have no doubt. I am terribly afraid that he recognized you or heard what you said."

"I should think so, for he spoke to me," replied the signora, whose black eyebrows had contracted during the abbé's harangue, with an expression of bravado. "But it matters little to me."

"I must go, signora," I said, rising; "by remaining another moment, I shall consummate your ruin. Since you know where I live, you will let me know your wishes ——"

"Stay," she said, detaining me by force. "If you go away, I lose my only means of exculpating myself. Don't be afraid, Lila. Don't say a word, I forbid you. Give me your arm, cousin," she added, raising her voice slightly, "and let us go."

"Can you think of such a thing, signora? All Florence knows me. You will never be able to pass me off as your cousin."

"But all Florence doesn't know me," she replied, putting her arm through mine and forcing me to walk with her. "Besides, I am *hermetically* veiled, and you have only to pull your hat over your eyes. Come! pretend you have a toothache! Put your handkerchief to your face. Quick! here are some people who know me and are looking at me. Be more self-possessed and quicken your pace."

Talking thus, and walking rapidly, she reached the church door, leaning on my arm. I was about to take leave of her and lose myself in the crowd that was coming out with us, for the mass was at an end, when Abbé Cignola appeared once more, standing on the porch and pretending to talk with one of the sacristans. His sidelong glance followed us closely.

"Isn't that so, Hector?" said the signora, as we passed him, putting her head between the abbé's face and mine. Lila was trembling in every limb; so was the signora, but her alarm redoubled her courage. A carriage with the crest and livery of the Grimanis drove up with a great clatter, and the multitude, who always gaze greedily at any display of magnificence, crowded under the wheels and the horses' feet. Moreover, the Grimani equipage always attracted a particularly large crowd of beggars; for the pious aunt was accustomed to dispense alms lavishly as she drove along. A tall footman at the carriage door was obliged to push them back in order to open it; and I walked on, still escorting the signora, still followed by Abbé Cignola's inquisitorial glance.

"Get in with me," said the signora, in a tone that admitted of no denial, and with a vigorous pressure of my arm, as she placed her foot on the step. I hesitated; it seemed to me that this last audacious stroke would inevitably be her ruin.

"Get in, I say," she repeated in a sort of passion; and as soon as I was seated by her side she herself raised the window, barely giving Lila time to take her seat opposite us, and the servant to close the door. In an instant we were driving at full speed through the streets of Florence.

"Don't be afraid, my dear Lila," said the signora, putting her arm around her foster sister's neck, and kissing her affectionately on the cheek; "everything will come out all right. Abbé Cignola has never seen my cousin, and it is impossible that he should have seen Signor Lelio distinctly enough ever to discover the fraud."

"Oh! signora, Abbé Cignola is the kind of man one can't deceive."

"Bah! what do I care for your Abbé Cignola? I tell you that I make my aunt believe whatever I choose."

"And Signor Hector will say that he didn't go to mass with you," I observed.

"Oh! as for that, I promise you that he will say whatever I want him to; if necessary I will convince him that he actually was at mass while he fancied that he was hunting."

"But the servants, signora? The footman looked at Signor Lelio with a strange expression, then suddenly started back, as if he had recognized the piano-tuner."

"Very good! you must tell him that I met *that man* in the church and bade him good-morning; that he told me that he had an errand to do in our neighborhood, and that, as I am very obliging, I offered to save him the trouble of going there on foot. We will set him down in front of the first country house we come to. And you can say in addition that I am very heedless, that my aunt has very good reason to scold me, but that I am an excellent young person, although a little wild, and that it grieves you to see me so constantly reprimanded. As they are all fond of me, and as I will give each one of them a little present, they will say nothing at all. Enough of this! can't either of you think of something else to say to me than lamentations over a thing that is done? Signor Lelio, how do you like this gloomy city of Florence? Don't you think that all these black old palaces, iron-bound to the very eaves, look exactly like prisons?"

I tried to carry on the conversation in an unconcerned tone; but I was very far from satisfied. I felt no inclination for adventures in which all the risk was taken by the woman, and all the wrong was on my side. It seemed to me that she treated me very inconsiderately in exposing herself thus for my sake to perils and disasters which she would not permit me to meet or avert.

I was so distressed that I remained silent in spite of myself. The signora, having attempted in vain to maintain the conversation, also held her peace. Lila's face continued to wear a terrified expression. We had left the city. Twice I observed that we had reached what seemed a favorable place to stop the carriage and set me down; twice the signora refused in an imperious tone, saying that we were too near the city and that there was still danger of meeting some acquaintance.

For a quarter of an hour we had not spoken a word, and the situation was becoming intensely disagreeable. I was displeased with the signora, because she had involved me, without my consent, in an adventure in which I could no longer proceed at my own pleasure. I was even more displeased with myself for allowing myself to be led into a series of childish exploits of which all the shame must fall upon me; for, even in the eyes of the least scrupulous of men, to seduce or compromise a girl of fifteen must always be considered an evil and cowardly performance. I was on the point of ordering the coachman to stop myself, when, on turning toward my travelling companions, I saw that the signora was weeping silently. I uttered an exclamation of surprise, and, moved by an irresistible impulse, I took her hand; but she abruptly withdrew it, and throwing her arms about Lila's neck, who was weeping also, hid her face on her faithful soubrette's bosom and sobbed as if her heart would break.

"In heaven's name, why do you weep in such heart-rending fashion, my dear signora?" I cried, almost falling at her feet. "If you do not wish to send me away in utter despair, tell me if this unlucky adventure is the cause of your tears, and if I can help to turn aside the consequences which you dread."

She raised her head from Lila's shoulder, and replied, glancing at me with something like indignation:

"You must think me a great coward!"

"I think nothing except what you tell me," I said. "But you turn away from me, and you weep; how can I tell what is taking place in your mind? Ah! if I have offended or displeased you, if I am the involuntary cause of your unhappiness, how can I ever forgive myself?"

"So you think that I am afraid, do you?" she rejoined, in a tone at once tender and bitter. "You see me weeping, and you say: 'She is like a little girl who is afraid of being scolded!'"

She wept more bitterly than ever, concealing her face

in her handkerchief. I strove to comfort her, I implored her to answer me, to look at me, to explain herself ; and, in that moment of confusion and emotion, my feeling toward her was so paternal and friendly that chance brought to my lips, amid the sweet names by which I called her, the name of a child who had once been dear to me. That name I had been accustomed for many years to apply, unconsciously as it were, to all the lovely children whom I chanced to caress. "My dear signora," I said, "dear Alezia ——" I paused, afraid that I might have offended her by giving her accidentally a name that was not her own. But she did not seem offended ; she looked at me with some surprise and allowed me to take her hand, which I covered with kisses.

Meanwhile the carriage was rolling on like the wind, and before I had had time to obtain the explanation which I sought so eagerly, Lila informed us that the Grimani villa was in sight and that we absolutely must part.

"What!" I cried ; "am I to leave you thus ? for how long a time must I eat my heart out in this horrible uncertainty ?"

"Come to the park to-night," she said ; "the wall is not very high. I will be in the narrow path that runs by the wall, near a statue which you will easily find by turning to your right from the gate. At one o'clock!"

Again I kissed the signora's hands.

"Oh! signora! signora!" exclaimed Lila, in a mild, sad tone of reproach.

"Do not thwart me, Lila," said the signora, vehemently ; "you know what I told you this morning."

Lila seemed utterly dismayed.

"What did the signora say ?" I asked her.

"She wanted to kill herself," sobbed Lila.

"Kill yourself, signora!" I cried. "You who are so lovely, so light-hearted, so happy, so dearly loved!"

"So dearly loved, Lelio!" she replied, in a despairing tone. "By whom am I loved, pray? only by my poor mother and by this dear Lila."

"And by the poor artist who dares not tell you so," I added, "but who would give his life to make you love yours."

"You lie!" she exclaimed passionately; "you do not love me!"

I seized her arm in a convulsive grasp and gazed at her in stupefaction. At that moment the carriage suddenly stopped. Lila had pulled the cord. I jumped out, and tried, as I saluted my travelling companions, to resume the humble demeanor of the piano-tuner. But the red eyes of the two young women did not escape the footman's penetrating glance. He examined me with the greatest attention, and, when the carriage drove on, he turned several times to look after me. I had a vague idea that his features were familiar to me; but I had not dared to look him in the eye, and it did not occur to me to try to recall where I had seen that coarse, pale, heavily bearded face.

"Lelio! Lelio!" said Checchina, when we were at supper, "you are in high spirits to-day. Look out that you do not weep to-morrow, my boy."

At midnight, I had scaled the park wall; but I had taken only a step or two on the path when a hand grasped my cloak. To guard against accident, I had provided myself with what, in my village, we call a "night-knife," and I was about to produce it when I recognized the fair Lila.

"Just a word, Signor Lelio, in great haste," she said in a low voice; "do not say that you are married."

"What do you mean by that, my dear child? I am not."

"It doesn't concern me," rejoined Lila; "but I beg you not to mention that lady who lives with you."

"You are on my side then, my dear Lila?"

"Oh! no, signor, certainly not! I do all that I can to prevent the signora from doing all these imprudent things. But she won't listen to me, and if I should tell her of the circumstance that might and should part her from you forever,—I don't know what would happen!"

"What do you mean? Explain yourself."

"Alas! you saw to-day what an excitable person she is. She has such a strange nature! When she is disappointed, she is capable of anything. A month ago, when she was taken away from her mother to be shut up here, she talked of taking poison. Whenever her aunt, who is really a great scold, irritates her, she has nervous paroxysms which amount almost to insanity; and last night, when I ventured to say to her that perhaps you loved someone else, she rushed to her chamber window, crying like a madwoman: ' Ah! if I thought so!' I threw myself upon her, I unlaced her, I closed her windows, I didn't leave her during the night, and she cried all night, or else fell asleep for a moment to wake with a start and run about her room like a lunatic. Ah! Signor Lelio, she makes me very unhappy; I love her so dearly! for, in spite of her outbreaks and her eccentricities, she is so kind, so affectionate, so generous! Do not drive her to frenzy, I implore you; you are an honorable man, I am sure, I know it; everybody said so at Naples, and the signora listened with passionate eagerness to all the stories of your kind deeds. So you won't deceive her, and since you love the beautiful lady whom I saw at your house——"

"Who told you that I love her, Lila? She is my sister."

"Oh! Signor Lelio! you are deceiving me! for I asked that lady if you were her brother, and she said no. You will think that I am very inquisitive, and that it is none of my business. No, I am not inquisitive, Signor Lelio; but I entreat you to be a friend to my poor mistress, to be like a brother to his sister or a father to his daughter. Just think a moment! she is a child fresh from the convent and hasn't any idea of the evil things that may be said about her. She says that she doesn't care for them, but I know how she takes such things when they come. Talk to her very gently, make her understand that you cannot see her in secret; but promise that you will call on her at her mother's when we return to Naples; for her mother is so good and loves her daughter so dearly that I am sure she would invite you to her house to give her pleasure. And then, too, perhaps the signora's madness will subside little by little. One can often change the current of her thoughts with amusements and distractions. I told her about the beautiful Angora cat I saw in your salon, which rubbed against you so while you were reading her letter that you had to kick her to drive her away. My mistress doesn't care at all for dogs, but she loves cats. She was taken with such a longing for yours, that you ought to give it to her; I am sure that it would keep her busy and cheer her up for several days."

"If my cat is all that is necessary to console your mistress for my absence," I replied, "there is no great harm done, and the remedy is simple enough. Be very sure, Lila, that I will act toward your mistress as a father and a friend. Have confidence in me. But let me go to her, for perhaps she is waiting for me."

"One word more, Signor Lelio. If you want the signora to listen to you, don't tell her that the common people are as good as the people of quality. She is tainted with her nobility. Don't form a bad opinion of her on that account, for it's a family disease; all the Grimanis are like that. But that does not prevent my young mistress from being kind and charitable. It is simply an idea she has got in her head, which makes her fly into a great passion when any one thwarts her. Would you believe that she has already refused I don't know how many handsome young men, and very rich too, because they were not well-born enough for her. However, Signor Lelio, agree with her at first on every subject, and you will soon persuade her of whatever you choose. Oh! if you could only persuade her to marry a young count who proposed for her not long ago!"

"Her cousin, Count Hector?"

"Oh, no! he is a fool, and he bores everybody to death; even his dogs begin to yawn as soon as they see him."

As I listened to Lila's prattle, my fatherly manner having put her completely at her ease, I led her toward the rendezvous. Not that I did not listen to her with profound interest; all these details, trivial as they were in appearance, were very important in my eyes; for they led me by induction to a better knowledge of the enigmatical personage with whom I had to deal. I must confess also, that they cooled my ardor to a considerable extent, and that I began to look upon it as a most absurd thing to be the hero of a romance in competition with the first plaything that might come to hand; with my cat, Soliman, or —who could say?—perhaps with Cousin Hector himself at the very outset. Thus Lila's advice was identical with the advice which I gave myself and which I was most desirous to follow.

We found the signora sitting at the foot of the statue, dressed all in white—a costume by no means adapted to a mysterious meeting in the open air, but for that very reason perfectly in harmony with her character. As I approached, she sat so absolutely still that she might easily have been taken for another statue sitting at the feet of the white marble nymph.

She made no reply to my first words. With her elbow resting on her knee and her chin on her hand, she was so pensive, so lovely, and her attitude so graceful and stately, draped in her white veil in the moonlight, that I should have believed her to be wrapt in sublime contemplation, had not her love of cats and armorial bearings recurred to my memory.

As she seemed determined to take no notice of me, I tried to take one of her hands; but she drew it away with superb disdain, saying in a tone more majestic than Louis XIV. ever had at his command :

"I have been obliged to wait!"

I could not refrain from laughing at that solemn quotation; but my merriment served only to increase her gravity.

"Do not stand on ceremony!" she said. "Laugh on; the hour and the place are admirably suited to that!'

She uttered these words in a tone of bitter indignation, and I saw that she was really angry. Thereupon, suddenly assuming a serious expression, I asked her forgiveness for my unintentional offence, and told her that I would not for anything in the world cause her one moment's unhappiness. She looked at me with an uncertain expression, as if she dared not believe me. But I began to speak to her with such evident sincerity and warmth of my devotion and affection, that she soon allowed herself to be convinced.

"So much the better!" she exclaimed, "so much the better! for, if you did not love me, you would be very ungrateful, and I should be very unhappy."—And as I gazed at her, utterly confounded by her words, she continued: "O Lelio! Lelio! I have loved you ever since the evening that I first saw you at Naples, playing Romeo, when I looked at you with that cold and contemptuous expression which disturbed you so. Ah! you were very eloquent and very impassioned in your singing that evening! The moon shone upon you as it does now, but less lovely than it does now, and Juliet was dressed in white as I am. And yet you say nothing to me, Lelio!"

That extraordinary girl exerted a constant fascination over me which led me on, always and everywhere, at the pleasure of her caprice. When we were apart, my mind threw off her domination, and I could analyze freely her words and her acts; but when I was once with her, I speedily and unconsciously ceased to have any other will than hers. That outburst of affection reawoke my slumbering passion. All my fine resolutions to be prudent vanished in smoke, and I found naught but words of love on my lips. At every instant, it is true, I felt a sharp pang of remorse; but it made no difference —all my fatherly counsels ended in loving phrases. A strange fatality—or rather that cowardice of the human heart which makes us always yield to the allurement of present joys—impelled me to say just the opposite of what my conscience directed. I gave myself the most convincing reasons you can imagine to prove that I was not doing wrong: it would have been useless cruelty to talk to that child in language which would have torn her heart asunder; there was still time enough to tell her the truth—and a thousand other things of the same sort. One circumstance which seemed to lessen the danger actually contributed to increase it: I mean Lila's presence. If she had not been there, my natural uprightness would have led me to watch myself all the more carefully, for the reason that anything would be possible in a moment of excitement, and I probably should not have gone forward a single step for fear of going too far. But, being sure that I had nothing to fear from my senses, I was much less careful of my words. So that it was not long before I reached the pitch of the most intense, albeit the purest passion; and, spurred on by an irresistible impulse, I seized a lock of the girl's floating hair and kissed it twice.

I felt then that it was quite time for me to go, and I walked rapidly away, saying:

"Until to-morrow."

Throughout this scene I had forgotten the past, little by little, and had not once thought of the future. The voice of Lila, who went with me to the gate, roused me from my trance.

"O Signor Lelio!" she said to me, "you didn't keep your promise. You were not my mistress's father nor her friend to-night."

"It is true," I replied gloomily; "it is true, I have done wrong. But never mind, my child, to-morrow I will make up for it all."

The next day it was the same story, and so with the next and the next. But I felt that I was more deeply in love every day; and the sentiment which, on the first day, was simply an inclination to fall in love, had become a genuine passion on the third. Lila's heart-broken air would have told me so plainly enough, had I not discovered it first myself. All along the road I reflected upon the future of that love-affair, and I returned home pale and distressed. Checchina soon found out what was the matter.

"Poor boy!" she said, "I told you that you would weep before long."

And as I opened my mouth to remonstrate, she added: "If you have not wept yet, you soon will; and there is reason enough. Your position is a pitiful one, and, what is worse, absurd. You love a mere girl whom your pride forbids you to try to marry, and whom your delicate sense of honor deters you from seducing. You do not wish to ask for her hand, in the first place because you know that if she bestowed it on you she would make a tremendous sacrifice, and would expose herself for your sake to innumerable discomforts, and you are too generous to accept a happiness which would cost her so dear; secondly, because you dread being refused, and are too proud to run the risk of being treated with disdain. Nor do you want to take what you have determined not to ask for, and I am very sure that you would much prefer to go off and be a monk than to take advantage of the ignorance of a girl who trusts you. But you must decide on something, my poor fellow, if you don't want the end of the world to come and find you sighing for the stars and throwing kisses to the clouds. Let dogs bay at the moon; we artists must live at any price and every moment. So make up your mind."

"You are right," I replied gravely. And I went to bed.

The next night I went again to the rendezvous. I found the signora excited and in high spirits, as on the preceding night; but I was taciturn and gloomy for some time. She joked me at first on my *carbonaro*-like manner, and asked me laughingly if I was thinking of dethroning the pope or reconstructing the Roman empire. Then, as I did not

reply, she gazed earnestly at me, and said, taking my hand:
"You are sad, Lelio. What is the matter?"
Thereupon I opened my heart to her, and said that my passion for her was a misfortune to me.
"A misfortune? how so?"
"I will tell you, signora. You are the heiress of a noble and illustrious family. You have been brought up to respect your ancestors and to believe that antiquity and splendor of race are all that there is in life. I am a poor devil without a past, a nobody, who have made myself what I am. And yet I believe that one man is as good as another, and I do not consider myself any man's inferior. Now, it is clear that you would not marry me. Everything would forbid it, your principles, your habits, your position in life. You, who have refused patricians because their families were not noble enough, would be less able and less likely than any other woman to stoop to a paltry actor like myself. From princess to player is a long way, signora. So I cannot be your husband. What is left for me? The prospect of a mutual passion, wretchedly unhappy if it were never gratified, or the hope of being your lover for a time. I cannot accept either, signora. To live together, overflowing with a passion always intense and never allayed, to love each other in fear and trembling, and to distrust ourselves as well as each other, is to subject ourselves voluntarily to suffering that would be intolerable because it would be senseless, hopeless, and aimless. Nor would I, even if I could, possess you as a lover. My happiness would be assailed by anxiety from too many sources to be at all complete. On the one hand, I should always be afraid of compromising your good name; I could not sleep with the dread of being the cause of great misery to you, or of your utter ruin; during the

day I should pass long hours looking out for accidents which might bring misery upon you and consequently upon me, and at night I should waste the time that we were together in trembling at the fall of a leaf or at the cry of a bird. Everything would be a source of alarm to me. And why should I thus toss my life to a multitude of empty phantoms, to be consumed? for a love-affair of which I could never foresee the duration and which would afford no compensation for the uncertainties of to-day in a sense of security for the morrow; for sooner or later, signora,—I must say it frankly—you would marry. And you would marry a man of noble birth and of great wealth like yourself. It would cost you a bitter pang, I know; I know that you have a generous and sincere heart; you would desire most earnestly to remain faithful to me, and your heart would rebel at the thought of uttering a word which would put an end to all my happiness surely, if not to my life. But the constant assaults of your family, the very necessity of preserving your reputation, would drive you to take that course in spite of yourself. You would struggle a long while, no doubt, and vigorously. Your love for me would still be gentle and tender, but less effusive; and I, witnessing your grief, as I am not the man to accept long and painful sacrifices without returning them in kind, should myself force you, by going away from you, to resign yourself to that necessary marriage, preferring to consecrate my whole future to sorrow rather than to change your destiny by a dastardly act. That is what I wanted to say to you, signora, and you must understand now why I am afraid that this love would prove to be a misfortune to me."

She had listened to me with perfect tranquillity and in absolute silence. When I ceased speaking, she did not change her attitude in any way. But, watching her closely, I fancied that I detected an expression of profound perplexity on her face. Thereupon I said to myself that I had made no mistake, that she was weak and vain like all the rest of her sex; that the only difference was that she was honest enough to recognize the fact as soon as it was pointed out to her, and that she would probably be honest enough to admit it. So I allowed her to retain my esteem, but I felt that my enthusiasm vanished in an instant. I was congratulating myself on my perspicacity and my firmness, when the signora rose abruptly and walked away without a word. I was not prepared for that stroke, and I was painfully surprised.

"What! without a single word?" I cried. "You leave me, perhaps forever, without a single word of regret or consolation?"

"Farewell!" she said, turning toward me. "Regret I cannot feel; and I am the one who need consolation. You have failed to understand me, you do not love me."

"I do not love you?"

"But who will understand me," she added, stopping, "if you do not? Who will love me, if you do not?"

She shook her head sadly, then folded her arms across her breast and fixed her eyes on the ground. She was at once so lovely and so despairing that I had a frantic longing to throw myself at her feet, and only a vague fear of angering her prevented me from doing it on the instant. I stood still, saying not a word, with my eyes fastened upon her, waiting anxiously to see what she would say or do. After a few seconds she walked slowly toward me, and, leaning against the pedestal of the statue, said with a meditative air:

"So you thought me cowardly and vain; you thought me capable of giving my love to a man and accepting his, without giving him at the same time my whole life.

You thought that I would stay with you so long as the wind held fair, and that I would go away as soon as it became adverse. How can you have thought so? For you are a steadfast, loyal man, and I am sure that you would not start upon any serious course of action until you had determined to go on with it to the end. Why, then, do you insist that I cannot do what you do, and why have you not the same good opinion of me that I have of you? Either you must have great contempt for women, or you have allowed yourself to be sadly misled by my levity. I am often foolish; I know that; but perhaps that may be to some extent the fault of my age, and it does not prevent my being steadfast and loyal. On the day that I realized that I loved you, Lelio, I determined to marry you. That surprises you. You remember not only the thoughts that I must have had in my position, but also my past words and acts. You think of all the patricians I have refused to marry because they were not noble enough. Alas! my dear friend, I am the slave of my public, just as you sometimes complain of being of yours, and I am obliged to play my rôle before it until I find an opportunity to escape from the stage. But I have kept my heart free under my mask, and, since I have been able to reason, I have determined that I would not marry except in accordance with the dictates of my heart. But I had to have some excuse for dismissing all those insipid and impertinent patricians to whom you refer. I found it in the prejudices common to my suitors and my family, and, wounding the pride of the former and flattering the pride of the latter at the same time, I took advantage of the antiquity of my blood to refuse the hand of men who, noble as they were, were still, I said, not noble enough for me. In this way I succeeded in getting rid of all my troublesome suitors without displeasing my family; for although they called my refusals childish whims, and offered my rejected followers apologies for my exaggerated pride of birth, they were none the less enchanted with it in the depths of their hearts. For some little time I enjoyed greater freedom by virtue of this conduct. But at last my stepfather, Prince Grimani, told me that it was time to make up my mind, and presented his nephew, Count Ettore, as the husband he had in mind for me. This new pretender was as unattractive to me as his predecessor—even more so perhaps; for his excessive imbecility soon led me to despise him altogether. The prince, seeing this, and thinking that my mother, who is a dear soul and loves me with all her heart, might aid and abet me in my resistance to his will, determined to part me from her in order to force me more easily to obey him. He sent me here to live with no one but his sister and nephew. He hopes that, being compelled to choose between ennui and my cousin Ettore, I shall end by choosing the latter; but he is sadly mistaken. Count Ettore is unworthy of me in every respect, and I should rather die than marry him. I have never said so as yet, because I loved nobody, and, taking one scourge with another, I had no more objection to that one than to others. But now I love you, Lelio; I will tell Ettore that I will not have him; we will go away together—to my mother; we will tell her that we love each other, and that we wish to be married. She will give her consent, and you will marry me. Do you agree?"

I had listened to the signora, from her very first word, with profound amazement, which did not cease when she had finished. Such nobleness of heart, such fearlessness of thought, such masculine audacity blended with such delicacy of feeling—all these united in so young a girl, brought up amid the most arrogant of the old aristocrats—aroused the warmest admiration in my own mind, and my surprise gave place to enthusiasm. I was on the point of giving way to my transports and of throwing myself at her feet to tell her that I was happy and proud to be loved by a woman like her, that I was burning with the most ardent passion for her, and that I was ready to do whatever she choose. But reflection checked me in time, and I thought of all the drawbacks, all the dangers of the step she proposed to risk. It was very probable that she would be refused and severely rebuked, and then what would be her plight, after running away from her aunt's house and openly taking a journey of eight leagues with me? And so, instead of yielding to the tumultuous impulses of my heart, I forced myself to be calm, and, after a few seconds of silence, I tranquilly inquired:

"But your family?"

"There is but one person in the world whose authority over me I acknowledge, and whose anger I fear to incur: that is my mother; and, as I have told you, my mother is as kind as an angel, and loves me beyond everything. Her heart will consent."

"O dear child!" I cried, taking her hands and pressing them against my heart; "God knows that what you propose to do is the goal of all my desires! I am fighting against myself when I try to hold you back. Every objection that I urge means the loss of one more hope of happiness for myself, and my heart suffers cruelly from all the doubts suggested by my reason. But to my mind, you, my beloved angel, and your future, your reputation, your happiness, are to be considered first of all. I should much rather renounce all hope than have you suffer because of me. So do not be alarmed at all my scruples; do not see in them an indication of calmness or indifference, but the proof of an unbounded affection. You say that you know your mother will consent because you know that she is kind. But you are very young, my child; with all your strength of mind, you do not know what abnormal alliances are often found between the most contrary sentiments. I believe all that you tell me of your mother, but can you be sure that her pride will not resist her love for you? It may be that she will think that she is performing a sacred duty by preventing your union with an actor."

"You may be half right," she replied. "Not that I am afraid of my mother's pride. Although she has married two princes, she belongs to the middle class by birth, and has never forgotten her own origin so far that she would consider it a crime for me to love a plebeian. But Prince Grimani's influence, a certain weakness which makes her always coincide with the opinions of those about her, and perhaps, to represent things in the worst possible light, the longing to obtain forgiveness for her own humble birth in the social circle in which she now lives, would prevent her from giving a ready consent to our marriage. So that there is but one thing to do; that is to be married first and then tell her of it. When our union is sanctified by the Church, my mother will never have the heart to turn against me. It may be that she will suffer a little, less on account of my disobedience, although her new family will hold her entirely responsible for it, than on account of what she will consider a lack of confidence on my part; but she will very soon be appeased, you may be sure, and, from love for me, will open her arms to you as to a son."

"Thanks for your generous offers, my dear signora; but I have my honor to preserve, no less than the proudest patrician. If I should marry you without your parent's consent, after abducting you, people would not fail to accuse me of the basest and most dastardly projects. And your mother! suppose that after we were married she should refuse to forgive us, all her indignation would fall upon me."

"I understand then that, before marrying, you desire to have my mother's consent at least?"

"Yes, signora."

"And if you were sure of obtaining it, you would hesitate no longer?"

"Alas! why tempt me? What answer can I make, being sure of the contrary?"

"Then——"

She paused abruptly, in evident uncertainty, and dropped her head on her breast. When she raised it, she was slightly pale and tears were glistening in her eyes. I was about to ask her the cause of them, but she did not give me time.

"Lila," she said in an imperative tone, "go!"

The girl obeyed regretfully, and stopped far enough away to be out of hearing, but not so far that she could not see us. Her mistress waited until she had gone, before breaking the silence. Then she took my hand with a most serious air, and began:

"I am going to tell you something which I have never told before to a living soul, and which I had fully determined never to tell. It relates to my mother, the object of all my veneration and all my love. Judge what it must cost me to stir a memory which might tarnish her purity and her fair fame in the sight of other eyes than mine. But I know that you are kind-hearted, and that I can speak to you as I would speak to God, without any fear that you will imagine evil."

She paused a moment to collect her ideas, then continued:

"I remember that I was very proud of my noble blood in my childhood. It was, I fancy, the obsequious fawning of our servants that planted that sentiment in my mind so early in life, and led me to despise everybody who was not noble like myself. Among my mother's servants there was one who did not resemble the others, and who had been able to retain, in his humble station, the dignity that befits a man. So that he seemed to me an insolent wretch, and my feeling for him was little short of hatred. Still I was afraid of him, especially after a certain day when I saw him watching me with a very grave expression, as I was running my loveliest dolls through the heart with a long black pin.

" One night, I was awakened in my mother's bedroom, where my little bed always stood, by the sound of a man's voice. That voice was speaking to my mother with a gravity that was almost harsh, and she replied in a griefstricken, timid, almost imploring tone. In my astonishment I thought at first that it was mamma's confessor; and as he seemed to be scolding her according to his custom, I listened with all my ears, without making a sound or letting them suspect that I wasn't asleep. They had no suspicion of me. They talked without restraint. But such an extraordinary conversation! My mother said: 'If you loved me, you would marry me,' and the man refused to marry her! Then mamma wept and so did the man; and I heard—ah! Lelio, I must be very fond of you to tell you this—I heard the sound of kisses. It seemed to me as if I knew the man's voice; but I could not believe the testimony of my ears. I longed to look; but I didn't dare to move, because I felt that I was doing a shameful thing in listening, and as I had even then some elevated sentiments, I tried not to hear. But I heard in spite of my efforts. At last the man said to my mother: '*Addio*, I leave you forever; do not refuse me a lock of your lovely hair.'—And my mother replied: 'Cut it yourself.'

"The care which my mother took of my curls had accustomed me to look upon a woman's hair as something very valuable; and when I heard her give him part of hers, I had a thrill of jealousy and grief, as if she had parted with property which she ought not to sacrifice to anybody but myself. I began to weep silently; but, as I had heard steps approaching my bed, I hastily wiped my eyes and pretended to be asleep. Then some one put aside my curtains, and I saw a man all dressed in red, whom I did not recognize at first because I had never seen him in that costume. I was afraid of him; but he spoke to me, and I recognized him at once; it was—Lelio, you will forget this story, won't you?"

"It was—signora?" I cried, convulsively pressing her hand.

"It was Nello, our gondolier—Why, Lelio, what's the matter with you? You are shivering, your hand trembles. O heaven! you blame my mother!"

"No, signora, no!" I replied in an inaudible voice; "I am listening attentively to you. This took place at Venice, did it?"

"Did I tell you so?"

"I think you did; and it was in the Aldini palace, of course?"

"Of course, for I told you it was in my mother's bedroom. But why this agitation, Lelio?"

"O my God! my God! and your name is Alezia Aldini!"

"Well, what are you thinking about?" said she,

testily. "One would say that you had just learned my name for the first time."

"Pardon me, signora, your family name—I always heard you called Grimani, at Naples."

"By people who were but slightly acquainted with us, doubtless. I am the last of the Aldinis, one of the most ancient families of the Republic, proud beyond words, and now ruined. But my mother is rich, and Prince Grimani, who considers my birth and fortune worthy his nephew, sometimes treats me sternly, sometimes wheedles me to prevail on me to marry him. When he has a kind day he calls me his dear daughter, and when strangers ask him if I am really his daughter, he answers, alluding to his favorite project: 'To be sure, for she will be Countess Grimani.' That is why I was always called by a name that is not mine at Naples, where I passed a month, and where I knew almost nobody, and why I am called by the same name in this region, where I have been living six weeks, and where I neither see nor know anybody."

"Signora," said I, making a mighty effort to break the painful silence into which I had relapsed, "will you please explain to me what relation this story can possibly bear to our love, and how, by the aid of the secret you possess, you can extort from your mother a consent which she would be otherwise disinclined to grant?"

"What do you say, Lelio? Do you believe me capable of such detestable scheming? If you would listen to me instead of passing your hands over your forehead with that bewildered air,—my friend, my dear Lelio, what new sorrow, what fresh scruple has assailed you in the last few seconds?"

"Dear signora, I beg you to go on."

"Very well! Understand that I have never forgotten

that incident; that it has caused all the sorrows and all the joys of my life. I realized that I must never question my mother on the subject nor mention it to anyone. You are the first person to whom I have ever told it, not excepting my dear nurse Salomé, or my foster sister Lila, to whom I tell everything. My pride suffered from my mother's error, which seemed to rebound upon me. However, I adored her just the same. Perhaps, indeed, I loved her all the more, the more I felt that she was weak and exposed to the secret maledictions of my relatives on my father's side. But my hatred for the common people increased in the same proportion as my love for her.

" My sentiments remained unchanged until I was fourteen years old, and my mother had apparently ceased to pay any heed to them. In the bottom of her heart she was pained by my contempt for the lower classes, and one day she made up her mind to reproach me timidly on that subject. I made no reply, which must have surprised her, for I was in the habit of arguing obstinately with everybody and on every subject. But I felt that there was a mountain between my mother and myself, and that we could not argue impartially on either side. Seeing that I listened to her reproaches with extraordinary resignation, she took me on her knees, and, fondling me with unutterable affection, talked to me about my father in the most unexceptionable terms; but she told me many things that I did not know. I had always retained a sort of enthusiastic respect, entirely without foundation, for that father of mine, whom I had hardly known. When I learned that he had married my poor mother solely for her fortune, and that, after marrying her, he had looked down on her because of her obscure birth and inferior education, there was a great reaction in my heart, and I soon hated him as intensely as I had loved him. My mother said many other things which seemed very strange to me and impressed me deeply, concerning the misfortune of marrying purely for convenience; and I fancied that I could see that she was not much happier with her new husband than she had been with him of whom she was speaking to me.

"This conversation made a profound impression on me, and I began to reflect upon the necessity of making marriage a matter of business, and upon the humiliation of being courted because of a name or a dowry. I resolved not to marry, and some time afterward, as I was talking with my mother again, I made known my determination to her, thinking that she would approve of it. She smiled and said that the time was not far away when my heart would feel the need of a different love from hers. I assured her of the contrary; but by slow degrees I came to realize that I had spoken rashly; for I was assailed by the most intolerable ennui when we laid aside our pleasant and secluded life at Venice, to travel about and mingle in the brilliant society of other cities. Then, as I was very tall and very far advanced for my years, it seemed as if I had hardly ceased to be a child before they were already talking to me about choosing a husband and about an establishment; and every day I overheard discussions as to the merits and drawbacks of some new suitor. I had not as yet felt the repugnance and terror which men without heart or mind inspire in well-born women. I was hard to suit. Having lived always with such a dear mother and been idolized by her, what a paragon of a man I must have met in order not to regret most bitterly her gentle yoke and her loving protection! My pride, already so irritable in itself, became more and more sensitive every day at the appearance of the vain, stilted, empty-headed creatures who presumed to pay court to me. I clung to the virtues of noble birth, because I had imagined up to that time that illustrious families were superior to others in courage, merit, courtesy and liberality. I had not seen the nobility except in the portrait gallery of the Aldini Palace. There my ancestors appeared before me in all their glory, with all their great feats of arms or pious deeds recorded on oaken bas-reliefs. This one had ransomed three hundred slaves from barbarian pirates and bestowed true religion and freedom upon them; that one had sacrificed all his property in war for the salvation of his country; a third had shed all his blood for her on some glorious field. So that my admiration for them was justifiable, and I felt that the blood in my veins was no less warm and generous than theirs. But how shockingly the descendants of other patricians seemed to me to have degenerated! They retained none of the qualities of their race except insufferable incompetency and sickening presumption. I asked myself what had become of the nobility; I found it only on armorial bearings and on the doorways of palaces. I determined to become a nun, and I urged my mother so persistently to allow me to enter a convent, that she consented. She wept bitterly when she left me there. Prince Grimani approved of my whim; for since he had unearthed, in some corner of Lombardy, a sort of nephew who might become rich at my expense, and bear magnificently, thanks to my dowry, the imperishable name of Grimani, his only thought was to make me obedient to his wishes, and he flattered himself that religion would make my character more pliable. What fervent piety, what a thirst for martyrdom one must have in order to accept Hector! They took me away from the convent three months ago; the fact is that I was dying with ennui there, and the rigid discipline to which I had to submit was beyond my strength. And then I was so happy to return to my mother and she to have me with her! But six weeks of convent life had wrought a great change in my ideas. I had come to understand Jesus, to whom I had always prayed with my lips alone. In my hours of solitude, in church, in the earnest outpouring of my heart in prayer, I had learned that the son of Mary was the friend of the hard-working poor, and that he had justly scorned the grandeurs of this world. And how shall I tell you? at the same time that I opened my heart to new sympathies, the thing that in my childhood I used mentally to call my mother's shame presented itself to me under very different colors, and I thought of it only with deep emotion. What took place within me? I cannot say; but I said to myself: 'If I should do as mamma did, if I should fall in love with a man of a different station in life from my own, the whole world would throw stones at me, all except mamma. She would take me in her arms, and hiding my blushes in her bosom she would say: ' Obey your heart, so that you may be happier than I was after breaking mine.'—You are touched, Lelio! O heaven! it was a tear that just fell on my hand. You are beaten, my dear! You see that I am neither mad, nor wicked; now you will say *yes,* and you will come and take me to-morrow. Swear it!"

I tried to speak, but I could not find a word; I was shuddering from head to foot. I felt as if I were about to faint. With her eyes fixed upon me she anxiously awaited my reply. For my own part, I was completely crushed. At the very first words of her story, I had been struck by its strange resemblance to my own; but when she came to those incidents which it was impossible for me not to recognize, I was completely bewildered and dazzled, as if the lightning had struck close beside me. A thousand conflicting and sinister thoughts took possession of my brain. I saw images of crime and despair fluttering about before me like ghosts. Deeply moved by the memory of what had been, appalled at the thought of what might be, I imagined myself the mother's lover and the daughter's husband at the same time. Alezia, that child whom I had seen in her cradle, stood before me, talking in the same breath of her love and her mother's.

A world of recollections crowded into my mind, and little Alezia appeared there as the object, even then, of a timid and unjoyful affection. I recalled her pride, her hatred of me, and the words she had said to me one day when she saw her father's ring on my finger. "Who can say," I thought, "that she has renounced her prejudices forever? It may be that if she should learn at this moment that I am Nello, her former servant, she would blush for loving me."

"Signora," I said to her, "you used, you say, to be fond of piercing the hearts of your dolls with a long pin. Why did you do that?"

"What do you care? why does that detail impress you particularly?"

"Because my heart aches, and your pins naturally came to my mind."

"I will tell you why it was, to show you that it was not a mere barbarous whim," she replied. "I used to hear it said, when a man did a cowardly thing, 'that's what it is to have no blood in the heart;' and I took that metaphorical expression literally. So when I scolded my dolls, I would say to them: 'you are cowards, and I am going to look and see if you have any blood in your hearts.'"

"You despise cowards bitterly, don't you, signora?" I

asked, wondering what her opinion of me would be some day if I should give way at that moment to her romantic passion. Once more I fell into a melancholy reverie. "What is the matter, in heaven's name?" said Alezia. Her voice recalled me to myself. I looked at her with streaming eyes. She was weeping too, but on account of my hesitation. I understood it at once, and I said, taking her hands with a paternal gesture:
"O my child! do not accuse me! Do not doubt my poor heart! If you only knew how I am suffering!"
And I walked rapidly away, as if by leaving her I could escape my unhappiness. On reaching home I became calmer. I went over in my mind the whole extraordinary succession of events; I worked out all their details, and thus banished from my own mind the flavor of mystery which had paralyzed me at first with superstitious terror. It was all strange, but natural, even to the Christian name, that name Alezia, which I had always longed to know and had never dared to ask.

I do not know whether another man in my place could have continued to love the young Signora Aldini. Strictly speaking, I might have done it without criminality; for you will remember that I had not ceased to be a chaste and obedient lover of her mother. But my conscience rebelled at the thought of that incest of the mind. I loved La Grimani with her unknown baptismal name, I loved her with all my heart and all my senses; but in truth I did not love in that way little Alezia, Signorina Aldini, Bianca's daughter, for it seemed to me that I was her father. The memory of Bianca's charms and fascinating qualities had remained pure and undimmed throughout my life; it had followed me everywhere like a providence. It had made me generous to women and brave against myself. Although I had since fallen in with many false and selfish beauties, I always had the certainty that there are those who are sincere and generous. Bianca had made no sacrifice to me, because I had refused to accept any; but if I had accepted it, if I had yielded to her enthusiasm, she would have sacrificed everything to me, friends, family, fortune, honor, religion, and perhaps her daughter too! What a sacred debt I owed to her! Had I paid it in full by my refusal, by my departure? No; for she was a woman, that is to say, weak and submissive, exposed to the implacable decrees and the bitter insults of irony. And she would have braved it all, she who was so timid, so gentle, so like a child in a thousand ways. She would have done a sublime thing; and I, had I accepted, should have done a dastardly thing. So that I had done nothing more than fulfil a duty to myself, whereas she had exposed herself to the risk of martyrdom for my sake. Poor Bianca, my first, perhaps my only love! how lovely she had always remained in my memory! "Why, in heaven's name," I said to myself, "am I afraid that she has grown old and withered? Ought I not to be indifferent to that? Should I still love her? no, probably not; but, whether ugly or lovely, could I see her to-day without danger?" And at that thought my heart beat so violently that I realized how impossible it was for me to be her daughter's husband or lover.

And then too, to take advantage of the past—if it were only by a silent assent to Alezia's wishes,—in order to obtain the hand of Bianca's daughter, would have been a dishonorable act. Weak as I knew Bianca to be, I knew that she would consider herself bound to give us her consent; but I knew also that her old husband, her family, and, above all, her confessor, would overwhelm her with their reproaches. She had been able to make up her mind to marry a second time, a marriage of convenience.

Therefore, she was at heart a woman of the world, a slave of social prejudices, and her love for me was simply a sublime episode, the memory of which was to her a cause of shame and despair, whereas it was my glory and my joy. "No, poor Bianca!" I thought, "no, I have not paid my debt to you. You must have suffered terribly, perhaps trembled with apprehension, at the idea that a servant might be peddling the secret of your weakness from house to house. It is time that you should sleep in peace, that you should cease to blush for the only happy days of your youth, and that you should be able to say, poor woman, on learning of Nello's everlasting silence, everlasting devotion, everlasting love, that there was a time in your fettered, disappointed life, when you knew love and inspired it."

I paced my room excitedly; day was beginning to break. In the lives of men who sleep but little, that is the decisive hour which puts an end to the hesitations conceived and nourished in the darkness, and which changes plans into resolutions. I felt a thrill of enthusiastic joy and legitimate pride at the thought that Lelio the actor had not fallen below Nello the gondolier. Sometimes, in my romantic democratic ideas, I had flushed with shame because I had left the thatched roof where I might have perpetuated a hardy, laborious, and frugal race; I had reproached myself, as for a crime, for having disdained the humble trade of my fathers to seek the bitter joys of luxurious living, the vain incense of glory, the false advantages and trivial labors of art. But by performing, in the tinsel of the actor, the same acts of unselfishness and true pride that I had performed in the rough jacket of the gondolier, I ennobled my life twice over, and raised myself above all false social grandeurs. My conscience, my dignity, seemed to me the conscience and dignity of the common people ; by debasing myself I should have debased the common people. *"Carbonari! carbonari!"* I exclaimed, "I will be worthy to be one of you." The cult of deliverance is a new cult; liberalism is a religion which should ennoble its followers, and, like Christianity in its early days, make the slave a free man, the free man a saint or a martyr.

I wrote the following letter to Princess Grimani:

"SIGNORA:

"The signorina has been exposed to great danger. Why did you, a loving and fearless mother, consent to send her away from you? Is she not at an age when any accident may decide a woman's future—a glance or a breath? Is not this the time when you should watch over her every instant, night and day alike, fathom her troubles, however slight, and count the pulsations of her heart? For you, signora, who are so gentle and so condescending in small things, but in great crises can always find in your heart so much vigor and resolution, the moment has come when you should display the courage of the lioness, who will not allow her little ones to be taken from her. Come, signora, come; take your daughter back, and do not let her quit you again. Why do you leave her in strange hands, subjected to injudicious guidance, which irritates her and would drive her into serious errors, if she were not your daughter—if it were possible for the seeds of virtue and of dignity planted in her breast by you to become the plaything of the first breeze that blows! Open your eyes; see how your child's legitimate and sacred inclinations are being thwarted, until you are in danger of seeing her resist wise counsels, and contract a habit of independence which it will be impossible to overcome. Do not permit a husband whom she detests to be forced upon her, and look to it that her aversion for him does not spur her on to make a rash and even more deplorable choice. Assure her liberty. Let her only chains be her anxiety concerning your enlightened love, lest, distrusting your energy in her behalf, she seek dangerous succor in her imagination. In heaven's name, come!

"And if you wish to know, signora, by what right I address this appeal to you, I will tell you that I have seen your daughter without knowing her name; that I have been on the verge of falling in love with her; that I have followed her, watched her, sought her acquaintance; and that she is not so well guarded that I could not have spoken to her and exerted—in vain, I doubt not—all the wiles by which an ordinary woman is seduced. Thank God! your daughter has not even been exposed to my rash advances. I learned in time that she was the daughter of the woman whom I venerate and respect above all the world, and from that moment her place of abode became a sacred spot to me. If I do not leave the neighborhood instantly, it is that I may be ready to reply to your most searching questions, if, distrusting my honor, you bid me appear before you and render an account of my conduct.

"Accept, signora, the humble respects of your devoted slave,
" NELLO."

I sealed this letter, wondering how I could forward it to its address with the greatest possible speed, and with no danger of its falling into strange hands. I dared not carry it myself, fearing that Alezia, in her irritation at learning of my departure, would do something foolish or desperate. Moreover, it was quite true that I wished to be able to open my heart completely to her mother when the time should come for me to confide everything to her; for I foresaw that Alezia would conceal from her no detail of our little romance, of which I had no right to tell the whole story except by her order. I feared, too, that the girl's enthusiasm would so prevail over her mother's weakness with the moving description of her passion, that the mother would eventually give a consent which I did not propose to accept. Both needed the help of my calm and immovable determination, and it might well be that when they were face to face I should stand in need of the strength they both would lack.

I had reached this point in my reflections when there came a knock at my door, and a man entered and approached me respectfully. As he had taken pains to take off his livery, I did not at first recognize him as the servant who had looked at me so closely on the day of the church episode; but as we now had plenty of time to scrutinize each other, we both involuntarily uttered an exclamation of surprise.

"It is really you!" he said. "I was not mistaken; you are really Nello?"

"Mandola, my old friend!" I cried, and I opened my arms. He hesitated an instant, then embraced me most heartily, weeping for joy.

"I recognized you, but I wanted to make sure; and so, at the first moment I have had at my disposal, here I am. How does it happen that you are called Signor Lelio hereabouts, unless you are the famous singer who is so much talked about at Naples, and whom I have never been to see? for I always go to sleep at the theatre, you know, and as for music, I have never been able to understand it. So the signora never makes me go up to her box till the end of the play."

"The signora! oh! tell me about the signora, my old comrade."

"I was talking about Signora Alezia, for Signora Bianca never goes to the theatre now. She has taken a Piedmontese confessor, and she has been entirely wrapped up in religion since her second marriage. Poor, dear signora, I am afraid that this husband hardly makes up to her for the other. Ah! Nello, Nello, why didn't you——"

"Hush, Mandola; not a word about that. There are some memories which ought not to come to our lips any more than the dead should return to life. Only tell me where your mistress is at this moment, and how I can send her a letter secretly and without delay."

"Is it something of importance to you?"

"It is much more important to her."

"In that case, give it to me; I will travel by post at full speed, and deliver it to her at Bologna, where she is now. Didn't you know it?"

"No, indeed. So much the better. You can be with her this evening, can't you?"

"Yes, by Bacchus! Poor mistress! how surprised she will be to hear from you! for you see, Nello, you see, Signor "——

"Call me Nello when we are alone, and Lelio before other people, until the old Chioggia affair is forgotten altogether."

"Oh! I know. Poor Massatone! But that is beginning to die out."

"What were you saying about Signora Bianca? That is what I am anxious to know."

"I was saying that she will turn very red and then very pale when I hand her your letter and whisper: 'This is from Nello! The signora remembers Nello, who used to sing so well!'—Then she will say to me in a serious tone, for she is no longer bright and cheerful as she used to be, poor signora: 'Very well, Mandola, go to the pantry.' And then she will call me back and say in a sweet tone, for she is just as kind-hearted as ever: 'Poor Mandola, you must be very tired!—Give him some of the best wine, Salomé!'"

"Salomé!" I cried; "is she married too?"

"Oh! she'll never marry. She is just the same, no older nor younger; never smiling, never shedding a tear, adoring the signora as always, and forever resisting her; very fond of the signora and always scolding her; kind-hearted at bottom, but not amiable. Has Signora Alezia recognized you?"

"No, indeed."

"I can believe it; I had much difficulty in recognizing you myself. People change so much! You used to be so small and so slender!"

"Oh! not too slender, if I remember aright."

"And I," continued Mandola with comical distress, "I was so active and graceful and quick and merry! Ah! how fast one grows old!"

I began to laugh when I saw how men delude themselves concerning their youthful graces as they advance in years. Mandola was very much the same Lombard giant that I remembered; he still walked sideways like a vessel beating to windward, and the constant balancing of the gondola as he rowed at the stern had caused him to contract the habit of standing on one leg at a time. You would have said that he was always suspicious of the level ground and was waiting for a wave to come to change his position. I had much difficulty in shortening our interview; he took great delight in it, and I derived a sort of sorrowful pleasure from hearing of that home where my heart had been thrown open to poesy, art, love and honor. I could not restrain a secret thrill of joy, overflowing with emotion and gratitude, when the honest Lombard told me of Bianca's long continued melancholy after my departure, her impaired health, her secret tears, her languor, her distaste for life. Then she had recovered her animation. A new love had touched her heart. A very charming man, of decidedly ill-repute, a sort of aristocratic adventurer, had sought her hand in marriage; she had been within an ace of believing in him. Being warned in time, she had shuddered at the dangers to which her peace of mind and dignity were exposed by her isolation; above all she had shuddered for her daughter, and she had fallen back upon religion.

" But her marriage to Prince Grimani?" I said inquiringly.

" Oh! that was the confessor's work."

" Well, there is such a thing as fatality, no one can escape it. Off with you, Mandola; here is some money, and here is the letter. Don't lose an instant, and don't return to the Grimani villa until you have spoken to me; for I have some important suggestions to make to you."

He left me. I threw myself on my bed and was just falling asleep when I heard the rapid footsteps of a horse in the garden upon which my window looked. I wondered whether it was Mandola returning because he had forgotten a part of his instructions. I overcame my fatigue and went to the window. But, instead of Mandola, I saw a woman in a riding habit, with her head covered with a thick black crêpe mantle which fell over her shoulders and concealed her whole figure as well as her face. She was riding a superb horse, steaming with sweat; and, leaping to the ground before her groom had found time to assist her, she talked in a very low tone to old Cattina, who had hurried to meet her, impelled by curiosity much more than by zeal. I trembled as I thought who it might be, who it must be ; and, cursing the imprudence of such a proceeding, I hastily dressed. When I was ready, as Cattina did not come to notify me, I rushed out into the hall, fearing that the reckless visitor might remain on the stoop exposed to some inquisitive eye. But I found Cattina at the foot of the steps, returning to her work after showing the stranger into the house.

"Where is that lady ? " I inquired eagerly.

" That lady !" repeated the old woman, "what lady, my *blessed* Signor Lelio ? "

"What trick are you trying to play on me, you old fool ? Didn't I see a lady dressed in black come in, and didn't she ask to speak to me ? "

"No, as I believe in baptism, Signor Lelio. The lady asked for Signora Checchina, and didn't mention your name. She put this half-sequin in my hand and bade me keep her presence a secret *from the other people in the house.* That's just what she said."

"Did you see the lady, Cattina ? "

"I saw her dress and her veil, and a great lock of black hair that had got loose and fell on a beautiful hand, and two great eyes that shone behind the lace like two lamps behind a curtain."

"Where did you put her ? "

" In Signora Checchina's small salon, while the signora is dressing to receive her."

" Very well, Cattina ; keep your mouth shut, since she bade you."

I was uncertain whether it was Alezia who had come to confide in Checchina. If so, it was my duty to prevent her, at any price, from remaining in that house, where every instant of her stay might contribute to the ruin of her reputation; but if it were not she, what right had I to go and question a person who, doubtless, had some very serious motive for concealing her actions in this way? I had been unable from my window to judge of the height of that veiled woman, because our respective positions were such that I could see only the top of her head. I had scrutinized the groom as he led the horses to a clump of trees which his mistress pointed out to him. I had never seen his face before; but that was no reason why he might not belong to the Grimani establishment, for I certainly had not seen all the servants. I disliked extremely to question him and try to bribe him. I determined to go to Checchina; I knew what a length of time she required to make the simplest toilet. She could not have joined her visitor as yet, and I could reach her bedroom without passing through the small salon. I knew the secret passage which connected Nasi's apartments with his mistress's, the villa of Cafaggiolo being a genuine *petite maison,* built according to the French style of the 18th century.

I found Checchina half-dressed, and making ready with queenly indifference for this early morning audience.

"What does this mean?" she cried, as I entered by way of her alcove.

"Just a word, Checchina," I said in her ear. "Send away your maid."

"Make haste," she said when we were alone, "for there is someone waiting for me."

"I know it, and that is what I came to speak to you about. Do you know this woman who has requested an interview with you?"

"How do I know? She refused to tell my maid her name, and at that I sent word to her that I was not in the habit of receiving people whom I did not know, at seven o'clock in the morning; but she wouldn't be refused, and she begged Teresa so earnestly—indeed it is probable that she gave her money in order to enlist her in her interest—that the girl came and bothered me to death, and I backed down; but not without the greatest reluctance to get up so early, for I read of the loves of Angélique and Médor far into the night."

"Listen, Checchina; I think that this woman is—the one you know about."

"Oh! do you think so? In that case, go and join her. I understand why she asked for me, and why you came here by the secret passage. I will be close-mouthed, and delighted to go to sleep again, and you will be the happiest of men."

"No, my dear Francesca, you are mistaken. If I had arranged an assignation under your auspices, be very sure that I would have asked your permission. But I have not reached that stage, and my romance is drawing to a conclusion—to the least ardent and most moral of conclusions. But this young woman is ruined unless you come to her assistance. Do not listen to any of the romantic projects which she has come here to confide to you; send her away at once; make her return to her people instantly. If by any chance she asks to speak to me in your presence, say that I am absent and shall not return during the day."

"What, Lelio! you are no more ardent than this, and she makes a fool of herself for you! The deuce! That is what comes of being conceited—one always succeeds. But suppose you are mistaken, *cugino?* Suppose this beautiful adventuress turns out to be not your Dulcinea, but one of the poor girls with whom every country swarms, who want to go on the stage in order to escape from cruel parents? Look you, I have an inspiration.

Let us go into the small salon together. If we push the screen before the door as we go in, you can creep in with me, keep out of sight, and see and hear everything. If this woman is your mistress, it is important that you should know at once just what is in the wind; and as I should have to repeat to you word for word what she says to me, it will be a much shorter way for you to hear it yourself."

I hesitated, and yet I was sorely tempted to follow that bad advice.

"But suppose it is some other woman," I objected; "suppose she has some secret to tell you?"

"Have you and I any secrets from each other?" said Checchina; "and have you less regard for yourself than I have for you? Come, no absurd scruples; come!"

She called Teresa, said a few words in her ear, and, when the screen was arranged, dismissed her and led me into the salon. I had not been in hiding two minutes before I found a break in the screen through which I could see the mysterious lady. She had not raised her veil, but I recognized Alezia's graceful figure and beautiful hands.

The poor child was trembling in every limb. I pitied her and blamed her; for the apartment in which we were was not decorated in the most chaste style, and the antique bronzes and marble statuettes which embellished it, although selected with exquisite taste as works of art, were by no means suited to attract the glances of an enamored girl or a modest woman. And as I reflected that it was Alezia Aldini who had dared to find her way into that heathen temple, I was, in spite of myself, more hurt than grateful for her action, because I still loved her a little.

Checchina, although she had dressed hurriedly, had

omitted nothing to accomplish the object so dear to women, of dazzling persons of their own sex by the splendor of their costume. She had thrown over her shoulders a cashmere *robe de chambre*, at that time a very rare object; she had surrounded her dishevelled hair with a net of gold and purple, for the antique was fashionable then; and over her bare legs, which were as strong and as beautifully moulded as those of a statue of Diana, she had drawn a sort of buskin of tiger's skin, which ingeniously supplied the place of the commonplace slipper. She had covered her fingers with diamonds and cameos, and held her brilliant fan like a stage sceptre, while the stranger, to keep herself in countenance, played awkwardly with her own, which was of simple black satin. She was visibly dismayed by Checca's beauty,—beauty of a somewhat masculine type, but incontestable. With her Turkish gown, her Median footwear, and her Greek head-dress, she must have resembled the wives of the old satraps who decked themselves out with the plunder of foreign nations.

She saluted her guest with a patronizing air bordering on impertinence; then, reclining carelessly on an ottoman, assumed the most Grecian attitude that she could invent. All this pantomime produced its due effect: the girl was utterly bewildered, and dared not break the silence.

"Well, signora or signorina," said Checca, slowly unfolding her fan, "for I haven't the slightest idea with whom I have the pleasure of speaking—I am at your service."

Thereupon the stranger, in a clear and somewhat metallic voice, with a very pronounced English accent, replied thus:

"Pray pardon me, signora, for disturbing you so early

in the morning, and accept my thanks for your kindness in receiving me. My name is *Barbara Tempest,* and I am the daughter of an English nobleman who has been living in Florence for a short time. My parents are having me take music lessons, and I have already acquired some talent; but I had a most excellent teacher who has gone to Milan, and my parents want me now to take lessons of that stupid Tosani, who will disgust me with the art with his antiquated method and his absurd cadenzas. I have heard that Signor Lelio—whom I heard several times at Naples—was coming to this neighborhood, and that he had hired this house, the owner of which I know, for the season. I have an irresistible desire to take lessons of that famous singer, and I asked leave of my parents, who consented; but they have spoken about it to several people, and have been told that Signor Lelio is a man of a very proud and somewhat eccentric character, that, in addition, he is associated with what they call *charbonnerie,* I believe, that is to say he has taken an oath to exterminate all the rich and all the nobles, and that he detests them all. He doesn't miss an opportunity, so my father was told, to show his aversion to them, and if he ever, by any chance, consents to do them a service, to sing at their parties, or give lessons in their families, he doesn't do it until he has made them implore him in the most humble terms. If they prove to him, by very earnest appeals, how highly they esteem his talent and his person, he yields and becomes amiable; but if they treat him as an ordinary artist, he refuses sharply, and is not sparing of his mockery. This, signora, is what my parents have heard, and it is what they fear; for they are a little vain of their name and their social position. For my own part, I have no prejudices, and I have such profound admiration for talent, that there is no price that I would not pay to obtain from Signor Lelio the favor of being his pupil.

"I have very often said to myself that if I could only have an opportunity to speak to him, he certainly would grant my request. But not only am I not likely to have an opportunity to meet him, but it would not be proper for a young woman to accost a young man. I was thinking about it this morning as I was riding. In my country, you know, signora, young ladies go out alone, and ride out attended by their servants. So I ride early in the morning, to avoid the heat of the day, which seems very terrible to us northern people. As I was passing this pretty house, I asked a servant whom it belonged to. When I learned that it was Count Nasi's, who is a friend of my family, I asked if Signor Lelio had arrived, knowing that the count had let it to him. 'Not yet,' was the reply ; 'but his wife came on ahead to prepare the house for him ; she is a very kind and beautiful lady.' Thereupon, signora, it came into my head to call upon you and interest you in my desire, so that you might give me the benefit of your powerful influence with your husband, and induce him to grant the request of my parents when they present it. May I ask you also, signora, to be kind enough to keep my little secret and to ask Signor Lelio to do the same ? for my family would blame me severely for taking this step, although it is, as you see, perfectly innocent."

She pronounced this harangue with such genuinely British volubility, jerking out her words, cutting short the long syllables, and drawling over the short ones, her Anglicisms were so natural and amusing, that I no longer believed that prudish yet reckless young lady to be Alezia. Checchina, for her part, thought of nothing but making merry over her eccentric performance. I would gladly have retired, as I was hardly in a mood to enjoy that amusement; but the slightest sound would have betrayed my presence and struck terror to Miss Barbara's guileless heart.

"Really, miss," Checchina replied, concealing a strong desire to laugh behind a phial of essence of rose, "your request is most embarrassing, and I don't know how to answer it. I will admit that I have not the influence over Signor Lelio which you are pleased to attribute to me."

"Can it be that you are not his wife?" inquired the young Englishwoman artlessly.

"Oh! miss, to think of a young lady having such ideas!" exclaimed Checchina assuming a prudish air that sat most awkwardly upon her. "Fie, fie! Does custom permit young ladies in England to make such suppositions?"

Poor Barbara was altogether bewildered.

"I do not know whether my question was insulting," she rejoined in a trembling but resolute voice; "I certainly did not so intend it. You could not live with Signor Lelio without committing a crime unless you were his wife. You might, perhaps, be his sister—That is all I wanted to say, signora."

"And might I not be neither his wife, nor his sister, nor his mistress, but be living in my own house? May I not be Countess Nasi?"

"O signora," replied Barbara ingenuously, "I know that Signor Nasi is not married."

"He may be secretly, miss."

"It must be very recently then; for he asked for my hand not more than a fortnight ago."

"Ah! it was you, was it, signorina?" cried Checchina with a tragic gesture which caused her fan to fall. There was a moment's silence. Then the young stranger, being determined to break it at any price, seemed to make a great effort, left her chair and picked up the singer's fan. She handed it to her with charming grace, and said in a caressing tone which made her foreign accent even more appealing :

"You will have the kindness to mention me to your brother, will you not, signora ? "

"You mean my husband ? " rejoined Checchina, accepting her fan with a mocking air and eyeing the young Englishwoman with malevolent curiosity. The visitor fell back in her chair as if she had received her death blow ; and Checchina, who detested society women and took a savage joy in crushing them when she was brought into rivalry with them, added as she surveyed herself absent-mindedly in the mirror over the ottoman :

"Look you, my dear Miss Barbara. I wish you well ; for you seem to me a charming person. But you should have told me the truth : I fear that it is not love of art which brings you here, but a sort of a fancy for Lelio. He has unconsciously inspired many romantic passions during his life, and I know as many as ten boarding-school misses who are wild over him."

"Never fear, signora," retorted the English girl, with an Italian accent which gave me a shock, "I could never have the slightest feeling for a married man ; and when I entered this house I knew that you were Signor Lelio's wife."

Checchina was a little disconcerted by the firm and contemptuous tone of this retort ; but, being determined to force her to the last extremity, she soon recovered herself, and said with a studied smile, and with redoubled impertinence :

"Dear Barbara, you set my mind at rest, and I believe that you are too noble-minded to wish to rob me of Lelio's heart; but I cannot conceal from you that I have one wretched failing. I am of a frantically jealous disposition and everything arouses my suspicions. You are lovelier than I, perhaps, and I am much afraid that it is so, judging from the pretty foot which I see and the great eyes which I divine. You will be indifferent to Lelio, since he belongs to me, for you are high-spirited and generous: but Lelio may fall in love with you; you will not be the first one who has turned his head. He is a fickle creature; his blood kindles for every pretty woman he meets. So pray be kind enough, dear Signora Barbara, to raise your veil, so that I may see what I have to fear, and, to use the French phrase, whether I can safely expose Lelio to the fire of your batteries."

The English girl made a gesture of disgust, then seemed to hesitate; and at last, drawing herself up to her full height, she replied, beginning to detach her veil:

"Look at me, signora, and remember my features, so that you may describe them to Signor Lelio; and if, as he listens to your description, he seems moved, do not by any means send him to me; for, if he should be faithless to you, I declare that it would be a most unfortunate thing for him, and that he would obtain nothing but contempt from me."

As she was speaking, she uncovered her face. Her back was turned toward me, and I tried in vain to see her features in the mirror. But what need had I of the testimony of my eyes? was not that of my ears sufficient? She had entirely forgotten her English accent and spoke the purest Italian in that resonant, vibrating voice which had so often moved me to the very depths of my being.

"I beg your pardon, miss," said Checchina, in nowise discomposed, "you are so lovely that all my fears are revived. I cannot believe that Lelio has not seen you already, and that you and he are not acting in concert to deceive me."

"If he asks you my name," exclaimed Alezia, violently pulling out one of the long pins of burnished steel that held the folds of her veil in place, "give him this from me, and tell him that my crest bears a pin with this motto: 'For the heart in which there is no blood!'"

At that moment, unable to rest under the burden of such contempt, I suddenly emerged from my hiding-place and rushed toward Alezia with a self-assured air.

"No, signora," I said, "do not believe my friend Francesca's jests. This is all a comedy which she has enjoyed playing, taking you for what you chose to appear, and unaware of the importance of her falsehoods; it is a comedy which I have allowed her to play thus far because I hardly recognized you, you imitated so cleverly the accent and manners of an Englishwoman."

Alezia seemed neither surprised nor moved by my appearance. She maintained the calmness and dignity in which women of rank surpass all other women when they are in the right. One who had seen her impassive features, lighted up little by little by a charming smile of irony, might well have believed that her heart had never known passion, and was incapable of knowing it.

"So you think that I have played my part well, signor?" she retorted; "that will prove to you that I had some vocation for the profession which you ennoble by your talents and your virtues. I thank you with all my heart for having arranged an opportunity for me to act before you, and I thank the signora, who has been kind enough to give me my cue. But I am already disgusted with this sublime art. One must carry into it a fund of experience which it would cost me too much to acquire, and a strength of mind of which you alone in all the world are capable."

"No, signora, you are in error," I replied firmly. "I have no experience of evil, and I have no strength except to repel degrading suspicions. I am neither the husband nor the lover of Francesca. She is my friend, my adopted sister, the discreet and devoted confidante of all my feelings, and yet she does not know who you are, although she is as devoted to you as to myself."

"I declare, signora," said Francesca, seating herself in a more becoming attitude, "that I have very little idea what is going on here, and why Lelio has allowed you to form such suspicions, when it was so easy for him to destroy them. What he has just said to you is the truth, and you do not imagine, I trust, that I would lend myself to an attempt to deceive you, if I were anything more than a placid and entirely unselfish friend to him."

Alezia began to tremble in every limb, as if she had an attack of fever, and she resumed her seat, pale and thoughtful. She was still in doubt.

"You were very cruel to her, cousin," I whispered to Checchina. "You took delight in inflicting pain on a pure heart, in order to avenge your foolish self-esteem. Ought you not to thank your rival, since she refused Nasi?"

Kind-hearted Checca went to her, took her hands familiarly, and sat on a hassock at her feet.

"My sweet angel," she said, "do not be suspicious of us; you know nothing of the honorable and attractive freedom of Bohemian life. In your social circle we are slandered, and our best actions are called crimes. As you have allowed Lelio to love you, it must be that you do not share those unjust prejudices. Be sure, therefore, that, unless I am the very vilest of creatures, I cannot conspire with Lelio to deceive you. I can hardly understand what pleasure or profit I could derive from it. So let your mind be at rest, my pretty signora. Forgive me for extorting your secret from you by my foolish jesting. You must agree that if we had allowed the signora marchesina to make sport of us actors, it would not have been in the natural order of things. However, it is all very fortunate, and it was an excellent and brave idea of yours. You might have retained your suspicions and suffered a long time, while now you are completely reassured, are you not, *marchesina mia*? And you believe that my heart is too big to betray you in such fashion, don't you? Now, my dear love, you must go back to your parents, and Lelio will go and see you whenever you choose. Never fear, I will send him to you myself, and I will see that he doesn't give you any more cause for grief. Ah! *poverina,* men are in the world to drive women to despair, and the best of them is not equal to the worst of us. You are a poor child, who do not know as yet what suffering is. It will come only too soon if you abandon your heart to the torments of love, *oimè!*"

Francesca said many other things full of kindliness and good sense. While Alezia was somewhat offended by her artless familiarity, she was touched by her kindness of heart and won over by her perfect frankness. She did not respond to Checca's caresses, but great tears rolled slowly down her pale cheeks. At last her heart fairly overflowed, and she threw herself, sobbing bitterly, into her new friend's arms.

"O Lelio!" she said, "will you forgive me for insulting you by such a suspicion? Attribute it solely to my unhealthy state of mind and body for the last few days. It was Lila who, thinking that she could cure me in that way, and wishing to prevent me from doing what she calls a crazy thing, confided to me last night that you were living here with a very beautiful woman, who was not your sister, as she had believed at first, but your wife or your mistress. You can imagine that I couldn't close my eyes; I revolved in my brain the most tragic and most extravagant projects. At last I concluded that Lila might be mistaken, and I determined to learn the truth for myself. At daybreak, while the poor girl, overcome by fatigue, lay sleeping on the floor in my bedroom, I stole out on tiptoe. I called the most stupid and blindly submissive of my aunt's servants, and ordered him to saddle my cousin Hector's horse, which is very highspirited, and has nearly thrown me a dozen times. But what did I care for my life? I said to myself: 'Alas! everyone is not killed who wants to be!' and I started for Cafaggiolo, without any idea what I was going to do here. On the way, I invented the story I ventured to tell the signora. Oh! I beg her to forgive me! I wanted to find out if she loved you, Lelio; if you loved her, if she had any rights over you, if you were deceiving me. Forgive me, both of you. You are so kind; you will forgive me and love me too, won't you, signora?"

"Dear *Madonetta!* I love you already with all my heart," replied Checchina, throwing her long bare arms about her neck, and hugging her until she nearly suffocated her.

I was anxious to put an end to this scene and to send Alezia back to her aunt. I begged her to expose herself to no further risk, and I rose to order her horse; but she detained me, saying vehemently:

"What are you thinking about, Lelio? Send the servant and horses back to my aunt. Order a postchaise, and let us go at once. Your friend will be kind enough to go with us. We will go to my mother, and I will throw myself at her feet and say: 'I am compromised, I am ruined in the eyes of the world; I ran away from my aunt's in broad daylight, without concealment. It is too late to repair the injury I have inflicted upon myself voluntarily and deliberately. I love Lelio and he loves me; I have given him my life. I have nobody left on earth but him and you. Will you curse me?'"

This determination threw me into the most horrible perplexity. I argued with her to no purpose. She was annoyed by my scruples, accused me of not loving her, and appealed to Francesca's judgment. Francesca suggested going with Alezia to her mother, without me. I tried to induce Alezia to return to her aunt, to write to her mother from there, and to await her reply before deciding upon anything. I solemnly promised to have no more conscientious scruples if the mother consented; but I was not willing to compromise the daughter; that was a detestable deed which I implored Alezia to spare me. Her reply was that, if she wrote, her mother would show the letter to Prince Grimani, and he would have her shut up in a convent.

At the height of this discussion, Lila, whom Cattina strove in vain to detain on the stairs, rushed impetuously into our midst, purple in the face, breathless, almost fainting. It was several minutes before she could speak. At last she told us in broken phrases, that she had outstripped Signor Ettore Grimani, whose horse luckily enough was lame, and could not jump the quickset hedges between the fields; but that he was behind her, that he had inquired all the way along what road Alezia had taken, and that he would arrive very soon. Through his means, the whole Grimani establishment was informed of the signora's flight. The aunt had tried to make inquiries quietly and to impose silence on Hector's frantic outcries, but all to no purpose. He was making so much noise about it that the whole province would be aware before night of his humiliating position and of the signora's risky performance, unless she herself set things to rights by going to meet him, closing his mouth, and returning to Villa Grimani with him. I agreed with Lila. Alezia could make her cousin do whatever she chose. Nothing was irreparable as yet, if she would mount her horse and return to her aunt; she could take a different road from that by which Hector was coming, and we would send somebody to meet him and throw him off the scent and prevent him from coming to Cafaggiolo. But it was all useless. Alezia's resolution was immovable.

"Let him come," she said, "let him enter the house, and if he dares to come as far as this we will throw him out of the window."

Checchina laughed like a madwoman at that idea, and upon hearing Alezia's satirical description of her cousin, she undertook to get rid of him unaided. All this boasting and insane merriment at such a crisis grieved me beyond measure.

Suddenly a post-chaise appeared at the end of the long avenue lined with fig-trees leading from the main road to Nasi's villa.

"It's Nasi!" cried Checchina.

"Suppose it is Bianca!" I thought.

"Oh!" cried Lila, "here comes the signora, your aunt in person, to fetch you."

"I will resist my aunt as stoutly as my cousin," replied Alezia; "for they are treating me shamefully. They mean to publish my shame, to overwhelm me with chagrin and humiliation, in order to conquer me. Hide me, Lelio, or protect me."

"Have no fear," I replied; "if that is the way they propose to act toward you, no one shall come into this house. I will go and receive the signora, your aunt, at the door, and as it is too late for you to go out, I swear that no one shall come in."

I ran hastily down stairs; I found Cattina listening at the door. I threatened to kill her, if she said a word; then, reflecting that no fear was sufficiently powerful to prevent her from yielding to the power of gold, I changed my mind, retraced my steps, and, taking her by the arm, pushed her into a sort of store-room which had only a small round window which she could not reach; I locked the door on her in spite of her anger, put the key in my pocket, and ran down to meet the post-chaise.

Of all the possibilities that we dreaded, the most embarrassing was realized. Nasi alighted from the carriage and threw himself on my neck. How could I prevent him from entering his own house, how conceal from him what was going on? It was a simple matter to prevent his betraying Alezia's *incognito,* by telling him that a woman had come to his house to see me, and that I requested him as a favor not to try to see her. But the day would not pass without his hearing of Alezia's flight and the confusion into which the Grimani household had been thrown. A week would suffice to make it known all over the country. I really did not know what to do. Nasi, being entirely at a loss to understand my perturbed air, began to be uneasy and to fear that Checchina, in wrath or in desperation, had indulged in some insane freak. He rushed upstairs; his hand was already on the knob of Checchina's door, when I held his arm, saying with the utmost gravity that I begged him not to go in.

"What does this mean, Lelio?" he said in a trembling voice, and turning pale; "Francesca is here and doesn't come to meet me; you receive me with an icy manner, and you try to prevent me from entering my mistress's apartment! And yet it was you who wrote me to return to her, and you seemed desirous to reconcile us; what is happening between you two?"

I was about to answer when the door opened and Alezia appeared, covered by her veil. When she saw Nasi she started, then stopped.

"I understand now, I understand," said Nasi, with a smile; "a thousand pardons, my dear Lelio! tell me to what room I shall go."

"This way, signor!" said Alezia, in a firm voice, taking his arm and leading him into the boudoir from which she had just came, and where Francesca and Lila still were. I followed her. Checchina, when she saw the count, assumed her most savage air, the same which she assumed in the rôle of Arsace, when she sang the soprano part in Bianchi's *Semiramis*. Lila stood at the door to forestall any more visits, and Alezia, putting aside her veil, said to the stupefied count:

"Signor count, you asked my hand in marriage a fortnight ago. The short time during which I had the pleasure of seeing you at Naples was sufficient to give me a more favorable idea of you than of any other of my suitors. My mother wrote, imploring, almost commanding me to accept your offer. Prince Grimani added, by way of postscript, that, if I really felt any aversion for my cousin Hector, he would allow me to return to my mother, on condition that I would instantly accept you for my husband. According to my reply, they were either to come and take me to Venice to meet you, or to leave me at my aunt's house with my cousin for an indefinite period. Very good! despite my aversion for my cousin, despite the constant teasing and pestering of my aunt, despite my ardent longing to see my darling mother and my dear Venice once more, and despite my very great esteem for you, signor count, I refused. You probably thought that I preferred my cousin.—Look!" she said, interrupting herself and glancing calmly toward the window, "there he is, actually riding his horse into your garden. Stay, Signor Lelio!" she added, grasping my arm as I rushed to the door to leave the room; "you will surely agree that at this moment there shall be no other will here than mine. Stand with Lila in front of that door until I have finished speaking."

I put Lila aside and kept the door in her place. Alezia continued:

"I refused, signor count, because I could not loyally accept your honorable proposal. I replied to the obliging letter which you enclosed with my mother's."

"Yes, signora," said the count, "you replied in a kindly tone by which I was deeply touched; but with a frankness which left me no hope; and I have come into your neighborhood not with the purpose of annoying you further, but of being your devoted friend and humble servant, if you ever deign to appeal to my sentiment of respect."

"I know it, and I rely upon you," said Alezia, offering him her hand with a nobly sympathetic air. "The time has come, sooner than you can have anticipated, to put your generous sentiments to the proof. My reason for refusing your hand was that I love Lelio; my reason for being here is that I am determined never to marry any man but him."

The count was so astounded by this avowal that for several minutes he was unable to reply. God forbid that I should speak slightingly of honest Nasi's friendship; but at that moment I saw plainly enough that among the nobles there is no personal friendship, no amount of devotion, or esteem, which can entirely eradicate the prejudices of the caste. My eyes were fixed upon him in the closest scrutiny, and I could read this thought clearly on his face: "I, Count Nasi, have actually loved and offered marriage to a woman who is in love with an actor and means to marry him!"

But it was all over in an instant. Dear old Nasi at once resumed his chivalrous manner.—"Whatever you have determined upon, signora," he said, "whatever commands you have for me in pursuance of your determination, I am ready."

"Very good," replied Alezia; "I am in your house, signor count, and my cousin is here, if not to demand my return, at all events to establish my presence here. He will be offended by my refusal to go with him, and will not fail to calumniate me, because he has no spirit, no courage, no education. My aunt will make a pretence of rebuking her son's loss of temper, and will tell the story of what she will delight to call my shame to all the pious old women of her acquaintance, who will repeat it to all Italy. I do not propose to try to stop the scandal either by useless precautions or by cowardly denials. I have called down the storm upon my head, let it burst in the sight of the whole world! I shall not suffer on that account, if, as I hope, my mother's heart remains true to me, and if, having a husband who is content with my sacrifices, I find also a friend who has the courage to avow openly the brotherly affection with which he honors me. As that friend, will you interfere to prevent any unseemly, *impossible* explanation between Lelio and my cousin? Will you go and receive Hector, and inform him that I will not leave this house except to go to my mother, and with the protection of your arm?"

The count looked at Alezia with a grave and sad expression, which seemed to say to her: "You are the only one here who can understand how strange and reprehensible and ridiculous the part you are making me play will appear to the world;" then he knelt gracefully on one knee and kissed Alezia's hand, which he still held in his, saying: "Signora, I am your true knight in life or in death." Then he came to me and embraced me heartily, without a word. He forgot to speak to Checchina, who stood leaning on the window-sill, with folded arms, viewing this scene with philosophical attention.

Nasi made ready to leave the room. I could not endure the thought that he was about to constitute himself, at his own risk, the champion of the woman whom I was supposed to have compromised. I insisted upon accompanying him at all events, and taking half of the responsibility on myself. To deter me he gave me divers excellent reasons taken from the code of fashionable society. I did not understand them in the least; indeed I was carried away at that moment by the wrath aroused in my heart by Hector's insolence and his dastardly purpose. Alezia tried to calm me by saying: "You have no rights as yet except such as I please to bestow on you." I obtained permission to accompany Nasi, and thus make my presence known to Hector Grimani, on condition that I should not say a word without the count's permission.

We found the cousin just dismounting, panting heavily and drenched with perspiration. He cursed at the poor beast in the most vulgar way, and struck him violently because, being unshod and having bruised his feet on the road, he had not galloped fast enough to satisfy his master's impatience. It seemed to me that this beginning and Hector's whole manner showed that he did not know how to extricate himself from the position in which he had recklessly placed himself. He must either show himself a hero by force of love and frantic jealousy, or cut an absurd figure by a display of cowardly insolence. His embarrassment was made complete by the fact that he had enlisted two young friends of his who were going out to hunt, and had insisted on accompanying him, not so much to assist him, probably, as to amuse themselves at his expense.

We walked up to him without saluting him, and Nasi looked him in the eye, with a cold stare, without a word. He seemed not to see me, or not to recognize me.

"Ah! is it you, Nasi?" he said, hesitating whether he should raise his hat or offer his hand; for he saw that Nasi was not disposed to offer him any sort of greeting.

"You have no cause for surprise, it seems to me, because you find me in my own house," replied Nasi.

"Pardon me, pardon me," replied Hector, pretending that his spur had caught on a superb rose-bush by which they were standing, and which he crushed with his whole might. "I did not at all expect to find you here; I thought you were at Naples."

"It makes little difference what you thought. You are here, and so am I. What is the difficulty?"

"Why, my dear fellow, I want you to help me find my cousin Alezia, who has the assurance to go out alone on horseback, without my mother's permission, and who is somewhere about here, so I am told."

"What do you mean by *somewhere about here?* If you think that the young lady you mention is in this neighborhood, stick to the street and look for her."

"But deuce take it, my dear fellow, she is here!" said Hector, compelled by Nasi's tone and by the presence of his witnesses to pronounce himself a little more clearly. "She is either in your house or in your garden,

I can see that he does it from gratitude for what I am doing for her."

"Do you really think so, my dear Checca?" I said, marvelling at her penetration and the great good sense which she displayed on great occasions, ridiculous as she was in trifles.

"I tell you I am sure of it. So they must be married. Let us leave them together. Let us go away at once."

"Let us go to-night; I agree to that," said I; "until then it is impossible. I will tell you the reason in two or three hours. Go back to Alezia before she wakes."

"Oh! she is not asleep," replied Checca; "she has done nothing but pace the floor in great agitation all night long. Her maid Lila, who insisted on sleeping in her room, talks with her from time to time, and irritates her exceedingly by her remonstrances; for, I warn you, she doesn't approve of her mistress's love for you. But when she begins to sigh and say: '*Povera Signora Bianca! povera principessa madre!*' the fair Alezia bursts into tears and throws herself sobbing on her bed. At that the soubrette implores her not to kill her mother with grief. I can hear all this from my room. *Addio;* I am going back. If you are fully decided to decline this marriage, think of my plan, and prepare to lend a hand to the poor count's love."

At eight o'clock in the morning we repaired to the battle-field. Count Hector handled his sword like Saint-Georges; and it was a good thing for him that he had had much practice in that detestable kind of argument, for it was the only kind that he had at his service. Nasi was slightly wounded; luckily, Hector behaved reasonably well; without apologizing for his conduct with respect to Nasi, he agreed that he had spoken ill of his cousin in the first outburst of his anger, and he requested Nasi

And how do you suppose that my mother, who is old and infirm, is to run about the country after a young madcap who rides like a dragoon?"

"I am certain, signor," retorted Nasi, "that your mother did not instruct you to search for her niece in such a noisy fashion as this, and to question everybody you meet in such an unseemly way; for if that were the case, her anxiety would be more insulting than protecting, and to place the object of such protection out of reach of your zeal would be a matter of duty with me."

"Very well," said Hector, "I see that you do not propose to give up our fugitive. You are a knight of the olden time, signor count! Remember that from this time forth my mother is relieved of all responsibility to Signora Aldini's mother. You may arrange this unpleasant business as you think best. For my own part, I wash my hands of it; I have done what I could and what it was my duty to do. I will simply request you to say to Alezia Aldini that she is at liberty to marry whomever she pleases, and that I will interpose no obstacle so far as I am concerned. I yield my right to you, my dear count. May you never have to seek your wife in another man's house, for you see by my example what an absurd figure one cuts under such circumstances."

"Many people think, signor count," replied Nasi, "that there is always some way to dignify the most uncomfortable position, and to compel respect, however ridiculous one may appear. One does not cut an absurd figure except as the result of an absurd action."

At this severe retort, a significant murmur from his two friends made it clear to Hector that he could not retreat.

"Signor count," he said, "you speak of an absurd

action. What do you call an absurd action, I pray to know?"

"You can give my words whatever meaning you please, signor."

"You insult me, signor!"

"That is for you to say, signor. It is none of my affair."

"You will give me satisfaction, I presume?"

"Very good."

"Your hour?"

"Whenever you choose."

"To-morrow morning at eight o'clock, on the plain of Maso, if that is agreeable to you. These gentlemen will be my seconds."

"Very good, signor; my friend here will be mine."

Hector glanced at me with a disdainful smile, and, leading Nasi aside, with his two companions, said to him:

"Come, come, my dear count, allow me to tell you that this is carrying the jest too far. Now that it has come to a question of fighting, we should be serious for a moment, it seems to me. My seconds are gentlemen of rank: the Marquis de Mazzorbo and Signor de Monteverbasco. I am sure that you would not associate with them, as your second, this person to whom I ordered my servant to give twenty francs the other day for tuning a piano at my mother's house. Really, I cannot stand such a thing. Yesterday, we discovered that this person has an intrigue with my cousin, and to-day you tell us that he is your intimate friend. Be good enough at least to tell us his name."

"You are utterly mistaken, signor count. This *person,* as you call him, does not tune pianos, and has never set foot in your mother's house. He is Signor Lelio, one of our greatest artists, and one of the best and most honorable men whom I know."

I had overheard indistinctly the beginning of this conversation, and, finding that I was the subject of discussion, had walked rapidly toward the group. When I heard Count Hector speak bluntly of an *intrigue* with Alezia, the dissatisfaction which I felt because the battle was being fought without me changed to indignation, and I determined to make some one of our adversaries pay for the falseness of my position. I could not vent my spleen on Count Hector, who had already been insulted by Nasi; so it was upon Signor de Monteverbasco that the storm fell. That worthy squire, on learning my name had said simply, with an air of amazement:

"The deuce!"

I walked up to him, and looked him in the eye with a threatening expression.

"What do you mean by that, signor?"

"Why, I said nothing, signor."

"I beg your pardon, signor, you said: 'That is still worse.'"

"No, signor, I did not say so."

"Yes, signor, you did say so."

"If you absolutely insist upon it, signor, let us agree that I did say it."

"Ah! you admit it at last. Very good, signor; if you do not consider me good enough for a second, I shall find a way to compel you to consider me good enough for an adversary."

"Is this a challenge, signor?"

"Call it whatever you please, signor. But let me tell you that I don't remember your name, and that I don't like your face."

"It is well, signor ; if agreeable to you, we will meet at the same time and place as these gentlemen."

"Agreed. Gentlemen, I have the honor to salute you."

Whereupon, Nasi and I returned to the house, after enjoining silence on the servants.

Hector Grimani's conduct on that occasion introduced me to a type of the men one meets in fashionable society, which I had not before observed. If it had occurred to me to pass judgment on Hector the first time I had seen him at Villa Grimani, when he retreated into his cravat and his nullity in order not to be intolerable to his cousin, I should have said that he was a weak, harmless, cold, but good-natured youth. Was it possible that such an insignificant creature could cherish a feeling of hostility ? Could those mechanically refined manners conceal an instinctive tendency to brutal domination and cowardly resentment ? I would not have believed it ; I did not expect to hear him demand satisfaction of Nasi for his harsh reception ; for I thought that he was more polished and less courageous, and I was astonished to find that, after being foolish enough to invite such a castigation, he had sufficient determination to resent it. The fact is that Hector was not one of those insignificant men who never do good or evil. He was ill-tempered and presumptuous ; but, being conscious of his intellectual mediocrity, he always allowed himself to be overborne in discussion ; then, spurred on by hatred and vindictiveness, he would insist on fighting. He fought frequently and always on some insufficient ground, so that his tardy and obstinate courage did him more harm than good.

Before I would allow Nasi to return to Alezia, I took him aside and told him that everything that had happened had come about against my wish ; that I had never intended to seduce or elope with or marry Signora Aldini, and that it was my firm determination to part from her instantly and forever, unless honor made it obligatory upon me to marry her, in order to repair the harm she had done herself on my account. I desired Nasi to decide that question.

"But before I tell you the whole story," I said, "we must consider the question that is most urgent at this moment, and take such measures that our young guest may be compromised as little as possible. I must tell you one thing that she doesn't know, that her mother will be here to-morrow evening. I propose to send a man to the first relay station, so that she may be told to come here directly and join her daughter, instead of looking for her at Villa Grimani. As soon as I have placed Signora Alezia in her mother's hands, I trust that everything will be straightened out; but, until then, what explanation am I to give her of the extreme reserve with which I propose to treat her?"

"The best way," said Nasi, "would be to persuade her to leave here and go back to her aunt, or, failing that, to go into a convent for twenty-four hours. I will try to make her understand that her position here is not tenable."

He joined Alezia. But all his excellent arguments were thrown away. Checca, faithful to her habit of boasting, had told the girl that she was Nasi's mistress, that the count had left her after a quarrel, and that it was then that he had proposed for Alezia's hand; but that, being fully cured by her refusal, and drawn back by an unconquerable passion to his mistress's feet, he was ready to marry her. So that Alezia considered that it was perfectly proper for her to be in Nasi's house, and she was overjoyed to learn that he, like herself, had made up his mind to yield to the craving of his heart, and to break with public opinion. She promised herself that she would find in that happy couple congenial companionship for her whole life and friendship proof against any trial. She was afraid of my scruples, if she left Nasi's house, and of the efforts of her family to reconcile her with society. So she obstinately persisted in ruining herself, and finally informed Nasi that she would not leave his house unless she was compelled by force to do so.

"In that case, signora," said the count, "you will permit me to take the course which honor enjoins upon me. I am your brother, as that is your wish. I accept that rôle with gratitude and resignation, and I have already acted the part by standing between you and Count Hector's insolent demands. I shall continue to act in accordance with the counsels of my respect and devotion; but if a brother's rights do not go to the extent of ordering his sister to do this thing or that, they certainly authorize him to put away from her anything that can injure her reputation. You will allow me therefore to exclude Lelio from this house until your mother is here, and I have just sent a messenger to her, so that you will be able to embrace her to-morrow evening."

"To-morrow evening?" cried Alezia; "that is too soon. No, I don't want her to come yet. Happy as I shall be to see my darling mother, I am determined to have time enough to be compromised in the eyes of society, and irrevocably ruined in its opinion. I insist upon starting off with Lelio to meet my mother. When it is known that I have actually travelled with him, no one will find excuse for me, no one will be able to forgive me, except my mother."

"Lelio will not comply with your desire, my dear sister," replied Nasi; "he will do just what I advise; for his heart is all delicacy and honor, and he has made me the final judge."

"Very well!" said Alezia, with a laugh; "go and order him, in my name, to come here."

"I will go to him," replied Nasi, "for I see that you are not disposed to listen to any prudent counsel. And I will go with him and take rooms for him and myself in the village inn, which you see at the end of the avenue. If you should be exposed to any fresh outrage on the part of Signor Ettore Grimani, you have only to signal from your window and ring the garden bell, and we shall be under arms instantly. But you need have no fear, he will not return. You can take possession of Lelio's room, which is much more suitable for you than this one. Your maid will remain here to wait upon you and bring me your orders, if it is your pleasure to give me any."

Nasi having joined me, and given me an account of this interview, I opened my heart to him and told him almost everything, but without mentioning Bianca. I explained to him how I had thoughtlessly become involved in an adventure, the heroine of which had at first seemed to me coquettish even to the point of impudence, and how, as I discovered from day to day the purity of her heart and the moral elevation of her character, I had been led on in spite of myself to play the part of a man ready to attempt anything.

"Then you do not love Signora Aldini?" said the count, in a tone of amazement in which I fancied that I could detect a slight touch of contempt for me. I was not hurt, for I knew that I did not deserve that contempt; and his esteem for me was restored when he learned how hard I had fought to remain virtuous, although consumed by love and desire. But when it became necessary to explain to the count how it happened that I was so positively determined not to marry Alezia, however indulgent her mother's heart might prove to be, I was embarrassed. I asked him this question : whether Alezia's reputation would be so seriously compromised by what she had done, that it would be my duty to marry her in order to make her honor whole. The count smiled and replied, taking my hand affectionately :

"My dear Lelio, you do not yet know how much rank idiocy there is in the social circle in which Alezia was born, nor how much corruption its stern censorship conceals. Let me tell you, so that you may laugh at such ideas and despise them as I do, that Alezia, after being seduced by you in her aunt's house and being your mistress for a year—provided there had been no noise or scandal about it,—could still make what is called a good match, and that no great family would close its doors to her. She would hear more or less whispering about her, and some rigidly virtuous women would forbid their newly married daughters to become intimate with her; but she would be all the more popular for that, and receive all the more attention from the men. But if you should marry Alezia, even though it should be proved that she had remained pure to the day of her marriage, she would never be forgiven for being the wife of an actor. You are one of those men upon whom calumny can gain no hold. Many sensible persons might think Alezia had made a noble choice, and done a praiseworthy thing in marrying you; very few would dare say so aloud, and even if she should become a widow, the doors that had been closed to her would never be reopened; for she would never find a man in society who would care to marry her after you; her family would look upon her as dead, and not even her mother would be allowed to mention her name. Such is the fate that awaits Alezia if you marry her. Reflect, and if you are not sure that you still love her, beware of an unhappy marriage; for it will be impossible for you to give her back to her family and friends after she has once borne your name. If, on the other hand, you feel confident that you will always love her, marry her; for her devotion to you is something sublime, and no man on earth is more deserving of it than you."

I was lost in thought, and the count feared that he had wounded me by his plain-speaking, despite the complimentary remarks with which he had tried to soften its bitterness. I reassured him.

"That is not what I am thinking about," I said; "I am thinking of Signora Bianca,—Princess Grimani, I mean,—and of the sorrow that would make her life a burden if I should marry her daughter."

"It would be very bitter, in truth," replied the count; "and if you know that amiable and charming young woman, you will think twice before exposing her to the wrath of those arrogant and implacable Grimanis."

"I will not expose her to it," I exclaimed earnestly, as if speaking to myself.

"I doubt if that resolution comes from a heart that is very deeply in love," said the count; "but it comes from a noble and generous heart, and that is much better. Whatever you may do, I am your friend, and I will uphold your decision against the whole world."

I embraced him, and we passed the rest of the day together at the inn near by. He made me tell him the whole story again, and the interest with which he questioned me concerning the most trivial details, the secret anxiety with which he listened to the narration of the perilous episode when my virtue had been put to the test, showed me plainly enough that that noble heart was deeply smitten with Alezia Aldini. While it made him wince to hear what I had to tell, it was evident to me that each new proof of courage and devotion which Alezia had given me quickened his enthusiasm and rekindled his love in spite of him. He constantly interrupted me to say: "That was fine, Lelio! that was fine! that was noble of you! If I had been in your place, I should not have had so much courage! I would commit a thousand follies for that woman."—And yet, when I gave him my reasons—and I gave them all to him, without, however, mentioning the love I had once felt for Bianca—he approved my virtue and resolution; and when I became sad in spite of myself, he said to me: "Courage, courage! Eighteen or twenty hours more, and Alezia will be saved. I think that we will treat the Grimanis to-morrow in such fashion as to take away any desire on their part to talk about the affair. The princess will take her daughter away, and some day Alezia will bless you because you were wiser than she; for love lives but a day, and prejudices have ineradicable roots."

We passed several hours of the night putting our affairs in order. Nasi bequeathed his villa to Checchina in case of emergency. The excellent creature's behavior toward Alezia had filled the count's generous heart with esteem and gratitude.

When we had finished, we snatched a few hours' sleep, and I awoke at daybreak. Someone entered my room: it was Checca.

"You have made a mistake," I said; "the next room is Nasi's."

"I am not looking for him, but for you," she said. "Listen to me: you mustn't marry this marchesina."

"Why not, my dear Francesca?"

"I will tell you. Obstacles and dangers kindle her

love for you; but she hasn't so much strength of mind, nor is she so free from prejudices, as she pretends. She is a kind, charming, lovable creature. Seriously, I love her with all my heart; but she has told me unconsciously, while talking with me, more than a hundred things which prove that she thinks that she is making an enormous sacrifice for you, and that she will regret it some day unless you appreciate its extent as fully as she does. And, tell me, can we actors, who are full of perfectly just prejudices against society, and despise it as much as it despises us, can we, I say, appreciate such sacrifices? No, no; the day would come, Lelio, I tell you, when, even though she did not sigh for society, she would accuse you of ingratitude at the first grievance she had against you; and it is a pitiful thing for a man to be the bankrupt debtor of his wife."

In three words I told Checca what my plans were with respect to Alezia. When she saw that I fully agreed with her, she said:

"My dear Lelio, I have an idea. This is not the time to think for ourselves alone, or at all events our thoughts even for ourselves should be noble thoughts, and such as to assure us a clear conscience for the future. Nasi loves Alezia. She has not been your mistress; there is no reason why he should not marry her; he must marry her."

I was not altogether sure that Checca was not impelled by a feeling of jealous disquiet to talk to me in that way, in order to make me talk; but she continued, giving me no time to reply:

"Be sure that what I tell you is true, Lelio; Nasi is wild over her. He is as melancholy as death. He looks at her with eyes which seem to say: 'If only I were Lelio!' And when he gives me any token of affection,

I can see that he does it from gratitude for what I am doing for her."

"Do you really think so, my dear Checca?" I said, marvelling at her penetration and the great good sense which she displayed on great occasions, ridiculous as she was in trifles.

"I tell you I am sure of it. So they must be married. Let us leave them together. Let us go away at once."

"Let us go to-night; I agree to that," said I; "until then it is impossible. I will tell you the reason in two or three hours. Go back to Alezia before she wakes."

"Oh! she is not asleep," replied Checca; "she has done nothing but pace the floor in great agitation all night long. Her maid Lila, who insisted on sleeping in her room, talks with her from time to time, and irritates her exceedingly by her remonstrances; for, I warn you, she doesn't approve of her mistress's love for you. But when she begins to sigh and say: '*Povera Signora Bianca! povera principessa madre!*' the fair Alezia bursts into tears and throws herself sobbing on her bed. At that the soubrette implores her not to kill her mother with grief. I can hear all this from my room. *Addio;* I am going back. If you are fully decided to decline this marriage, think of my plan, and prepare to lend a hand to the poor count's love."

At eight o'clock in the morning we repaired to the battle-field. Count Hector handled his sword like Saint-Georges; and it was a good thing for him that he had had much practice in that detestable kind of argument, for it was the only kind that he had at his service. Nasi was slightly wounded; luckily, Hector behaved reasonably well; without apologizing for his conduct with respect to Nasi, he agreed that he had spoken ill of his cousin in the first outburst of his anger, and he requested Nasi to beg her pardon in his behalf. He concluded by asking his two friends to give him their word of honor to keep the whole affair a profound secret, and they gave it. As Nasi and I acted as seconds for each other, he refused to leave the field until I had fought. His servant dressed his wound on the spot, and the battle between Signor de Monteverbasco and myself began. I wounded him quite severely, but not mortally, and when his physician had taken him away in his carriage, Nasi and I returned to the villa. As he did not wish it to be known at the inn that he was wounded, he was taken to the summer-house in his garden. Checchina, being secretly informed of what had taken place, joined us there, and gave him such care as his condition demanded. When he was able to show himself, he asked Checchina to tell Alezia that he had had a fall from his horse; then he appeared and bade her good-morning. But old Cattina, who had been released, and who, despite the lesson she had received, could not refrain from prying into everything, in order to gossip with all the neighbors, knew that we had fought, and had already told Alezia, who threw herself into the count's arms as soon as he entered the salon. When she had thanked him with the most effusive warmth, she asked where I was. In vain did the count reply that I was under arrest in the summer-house by his order; she persisted in believing that I was dangerously wounded and that they were trying to conceal the fact from her. She threatened to go down to the garden to find out for herself. The count was exceedingly anxious that she should do nothing imprudent before the servants. He preferred to come after me and take me to her. Thereupon Alezia, undisturbed by the presence of Nasi and Checca, reproached me warmly for what she called my exaggerated scruples.

"You cannot love me very much," she said, "since you refuse to assist me when I am absolutely determined to compromise myself for you."

She said the wildest and most loving words to me, but did not once lose the exquisite instinct of modesty which belongs to all young girls not absolutely devoid of mind. Checchina, who listened to this dialogue from an artistic standpoint, was utterly amazed, so she told me afterward, *della parte della marchesina.* As for Nasi, a score of times I surprised his melancholy gaze fixed upon Alezia and myself with indescribable emotion.

Alezia's vehemence became decidedly embarrassing. She called me cold, constrained; she declared that there was no joy, that is to say, no frankness in my glance. She took alarm at my conduct, she waxed indignant at my lack of courage. She was intensely excited, she was as lovely as Domenichino's sibyl. I was very miserable at that moment, for my love reawoke, and I realized the full extent of the sacrifice I must make.

A carriage drove into the garden, and we did not hear it, we were talking so earnestly. Suddenly the door opened and Princess Grimani appeared.

Alezia uttered a piercing shriek and rushed into her mother's arms, who held her there a long time without speaking; then she fell gasping upon a chair. Her daughter and Lila knelt at her feet and covered her with caresses. I do not know what Nasi said to her, nor what she replied as she pressed his hand. I was rooted to the spot where I stood; I saw Bianca again after ten years. How changed she was! but how touchingly beautiful she still seemed to me, despite the loss of her early bloom!

Her great blue eyes, sunken in their orbits which tears had deepened, seemed even softer and sweeter than I remembered them. Her pallor moved me deeply, and her figure, more slender and slightly bent, seemed to me better suited to that loving, weary heart. She did not recognize me; and when Nasi called me by name she seemed surprised; for the name Lelio told her nothing. At last I decided to speak to her; but she had no sooner heard the first word than she sprang to her feet, recognizing me by my voice, and held out her arms to me, crying:

"O my dear Nello!"

"Nello!" cried Alezia, rising hastily; "Nello the gondolier?"

"Did you not know him?" said her mother; "haven't you recognized him until this moment?"

"Ah! I understand," said Alezia in a stifled voice, "I understand why he cannot love me!"

And she fell at full length on the floor in a swoon.

I passed the rest of the day in the salon with Nasi and Checca. Alezia was in bed, wildly hysterical and delirious. Her mother alone was with her. We were all very melancholy at supper. At last, about ten o'clock, Bianca came and told us that her daughter was calmer, and that she would soon return and talk with me. About midnight she returned, and we passed two hours together, while Nasi and Checca sat with Alezia, who was much better and had asked to see them. Bianca was as lovely as an angel with me. Under any other circumstances she might, perhaps, have been embarrassed by her title of princess and her new social position; but motherly affection stifled all other feelings. She thought of nothing but expressing her gratitude to me; she did so in the most flattering terms and with the most affectionate manner imaginable. She did not seem to have dreamed for a single instant that I could hesitate to give her daughter back to her and put aside all thought of marrying her. I was grateful to her for it. It was the only way in which she gave me to understand that the past was still living in her memory. I had the delicacy to refrain from alluding to it; however, I should have been very happy if she had not feared to talk of it with perfect freedom; it would have been a greater token of esteem than all the rest.

Doubtless Alezia had told her everything; doubtless she had made a general confession of all the thoughts of her whole life, from the night on which she had surprised her love-affair with the gondolier down to that on which she had confided that secret to Lelio, the actor. Doubtless the mutual suffering caused by such an outpouring of the heart had been purified by the flame of maternal and filial love. Bianca told me that her daughter was calm and resigned, and that she hoped to see me *some day* and express her unchangeable affection, her great esteem, her cordial gratitude —— In a word, the sacrifice was consummated.

I did not leave the princess until I had told her of my earnest hope that Alezia would some day accept Nasi's love, and I urged her to cultivate the present inclinations of that honorable and excellent young man.

I returned to my inn at four o'clock in the morning. I found Nasi there; he had, in accordance with my instructions, made all necessary preparations for my departure. When I appeared with Francesca, he thought that she had come to see me off and bid me good-bye. Imagine his surprise when she embraced him and said, in a truly imperial tone:

"Be free, Nasi! win Alezia's love; I give you back your promise and remain your friend."

"Lelio," he cried, "so you are robbing me of her too?"

THE LAST OF THE ALDINIS

"Do you not trust my honor?" I said. "Haven't I given you proofs enough of it since yesterday? And do you doubt Francesca's grandeur of soul?"

He threw himself into our arms, weeping. We entered our carriage just at sunrise. As we passed Villa Nasi, a blind was cautiously opened and a woman leaned out to look after us. She had one hand on her heart, the other she waved to me by way of farewell, and raised her eyes to heaven to express her thanks: it was Bianca.

Three months later, Checca and I arrived at Venice one lovely evening in autumn. We had an engagement at La Fenice, and we took rooms on the Grand Canal, at the best hotel in the city. We passed the first hours after our arrival unpacking our trunks and putting our stage wardrobe in order. Not until that was done did we dine. It was quite late. At dessert they brought me several packages of letters, one of which caught my eye at once. After looking through it, I opened the window on the balcony, called to Checca to go out with me, and told her to look across the canal. Among the numerous palaces which cast their shadows on the placid water, there was one, directly opposite our apartments, easily distinguishable by its size and its antiquity. It had been magnificently restored. Everything about it had a festive air. Through the windows we could see, by the light of countless candles, superb bouquets and gorgeous curtains, and we could hear the melodious strains of a large orchestra. Gondolas, brilliantly illuminated, glided silently along the Grand Canal and deposited at the palace door women bedecked with flowers and gleaming jewels, and their escorts in ceremonious costume.

"Do you know," I asked Checca, "what palace this is opposite us, and the occasion of this party?"

"No, and I am not at all curious."

"It is the Aldini Palace, where the marriage of Alezia Aldini and Count Nasi is being celebrated."

"Bah!" she said, with a half-surprised, half-indifferent air.

I showed her the packet I had received. It was from Nasi. It contained two invitations and two letters, one from Nasi to her, one from Alezia to me, both charming.

"You see," I continued, when Checca had finished hers, "that we have no reason to complain of their treatment of us. These letters followed us to Florence and to Milan, and our constant journeyings are to blame for their not having reached us until now. And the letters are as kind and agreeable as it is possible for them to be. It is easy to see that they were dictated by noble hearts. Great nobles as they are, they are not afraid to speak to us, one of his friendship, the other of her gratitude."

"Yes, but meanwhile they don't invite us to their wedding."

"In the first place, they don't know that we are here; and in the second place, my dear sister, the rich people and the nobles do not invite singers to their parties, except to have them sing; and those who don't choose to sing to entertain their hosts are not invited at all. That is the justice of society; and kind hearted and sensible as our young friends are, as they live in that society, they are obliged to submit to its laws."

"Faith! so much the worse for them, my dear Lelio! Let them do as they please. They leave us to amuse ourselves without them, let us leave them to be bored to death without us. Let us snap our fingers at the pride of the great, laugh at their follies, spend money merrily when we have it, and accept poverty cheerfully if it comes; above all things, let us cling to our liberty, let us enjoy life while we can, and long live Bohemia!"

Here Lelio's story came to an end. When he had ceased to speak, none of us broke the melancholy silence. Our friend seemed even more depressed than the rest of us. Suddenly he raised his head, which he had rested on his hand, and said:

"On the last evening that I referred to, there were many French people among the guests; and as they were infatuated with German music, they made the orchestra play Weber's and Beethoven's waltzes all the evening. That is why those waltzes are so dear to me; they always recall a period of my life which I shall never cease to regret, despite the suffering with which it was filled. You must admit, my friends, that destiny has been very cruel to me, in placing in my path two passions so ardent, so sincere, so self-sacrificing, and not permitting me to enjoy either of them. Alas! my time has passed now, and I shall never again know aught of those noble passions of which one must have drained at least one to the dregs in order to be able to say that he has known life."

"Do not complain," said Beppa, aroused by her companion's melancholy; "you have an irreproachable life behind you, fair renown and kind friends around you, and independence in the future and forever; and I tell you that love will not fail you when you seek it. So fill your glass once more with this generous wine, drink gayly with us, and lead us as we sing the sacred refrain in chorus."

Lelio hesitated a moment, filled his glass, and heaved a deep sigh; then a gleam of youth and merriment flashed from his fine black eyes, moist with tears, and he sang in a resounding voice, to which we answered in chorus:

"Long live Bohemia!"